The First Lady

By Dan Dilbert

Other book by Dan Dilbert

ETHOS

The distinguishing character, sentiment, moral nature, or guiding beliefs of a person, group, or institution. (Webster)

Dan Dilbert

The distinguishing character of two men on a collision course based on their morale values. Joseph Dillward is a young, black college student in Maza City, North Carolina, who loves his family and determines to do the right thing. Phillip Goldwater, a white male, once CEO of Breachwind, the world's largest, most powerful corporation, leads an effort to kill Joseph and his entire family. Why? Because Phillip has discovered that the Dillward family can lay claim to a fortune from having invested in Breachwind since the end of the American Civil War – and can also insist that Joseph be made Breachwind new CEO.

Thank you for purchasing this book!

Please take the time to leave an honest feedback online. I do care to hear what you and others have to say, positive or negative, it will help me to be a better writer.

*****

The First Lady

*****

PUBLISHED BY:

Dan Dilbert on CreateSpace

*****

<u>DEDICATIONS</u>

This book is dedicated to you, the reader, and thank you for the support.

To my parents, Arthur Peter and Daisy Mae Dilbert, I love you both and proud to be your son.

ACKNOWLEDGEMENTS

I cannot express enough thanks to Danny Golshan for granting me permission to use such a beautiful picture, the model on the cover and to Baby Fresh Design for designing such an awesome cover for this book, thank you.

The completion of this project could not have been accomplished without the support of my test readers and their feedback, thank you Ruby Speights—the First Lady of Neabsco Baptist Church, Mae Ridges and my wife, VyVyonne Dilbert.

My sister-in-law, Sharon Murrell Dilbert for being a wonderful daughter of our Lord Jesus Christ, a loveable and supportive wife, a great mother, a role model for all women to model after and the First Lady of Abundant Life Faith Center Inc, The gifts the Lord has giving you is truly shining from the mountaintop.

To my caring, loving, and supportive wife, VyVyonne: I thank God for bringing you into my life. Your encouragement and choice words are duly noted. In the vastness of space and immensity of time, it is my joy to spend a planet and an epoch with you. Thank you for the positive and negative feedback you always provide. Know that you are loved!

I thank my Lord Jesus Christ for blessing me with a sound mind; I know without the Lord Jesus, I would be nothing.

OVERVIEW

Abundant Truth Baptist Church located in Jacksonville, Florida meticulously searched the corners of the United States for the perfect pastor; one that will serve the Church and the community by feeding and leading the flock through sound Biblical preaching, teaching and counseling, as well as a preacher after the heart of the Lord Jesus.

After a year beyond schedule and spending three times the allowable budget the church was forced to make a selection. Although 90% of the members voted for Pastor Jerome Samiah McCoy to be the Pastor of Abundant Truth Baptist Church, they are ready for him to leave and return where he came from, after his first day in Jacksonville, Florida.

The leaders of Abundant Truth Baptist Church quickly noticed that their newly non-selected First Lady, Joanne Sharnary McCoy, who befriended the most unpopular citizens *(homeless and gays)* in Jacksonville has became a force to be reckoned with, the members love and fear her, and they all give her the highest reverence.

Contents

Chapter One
The Culinary

"**M**edium caramel flan latte with whipped cream," yelled the young, petite, blonde lady wearing a green apron behind the Starbucks counter.

Beverly Lots, head of the Culinary Ministry at Abundant Truth Baptist Church, placed her Sunday-school book on the table, rose from her chair, quickly walked toward the counter, and received her drink. "Thank you," Beverly said to the young lady behind the counter as she accepted her latte. Then she returned to her table and comfortable chair and continued reading the Sunday-school lesson for the coming Sunday. She had chosen to sit in the far corner at Starbucks.

Abundant Truth Baptist Church was located on the North side of Jacksonville, Florida, around the 500 block of Kings Road. Beverly had been a member for about 10 years and had served as head of the Culinary Ministry for the past three years. Prior to the new pastor's arrival there, she had received no complaints regarding the services she provided to the good members of the church. It was Thursday afternoon and she was preparing herself for a long and busy Sunday.

While reading her Sunday-school lesson, Beverly noticed a biker had entered the parking lot. The rider slowly drove to the parking space directly in front of the window next to where she was sitting. Beverly had a flashback about her former days when she was young and reckless, hanging out with a group of bikers who only lived for the moment. That was years ago before she gave her life to Jesus.

The Culinary

Beverly began to reminisce about the days when she owned a 1990 Honda Nighthawk 250 and rode with the love of her life in Jackson, Mississippi. Her parents didn't approve of the young man she rode with. They told her a million times he was up to no good and not ready for a family. Beverly was not thinking about a family, she just wanted to be with Bernard Williams. No matter what her parents told her, she was going to be with him. Their relationship lasted four years.

One summer, they took a bike trip from Jackson, Mississippi to Los Angeles, California. Beverly and Bernard were putting Mississippi and all of the negative people in their lives behind them. The 1,842-mile trip took the couple three months. They took their time visiting friends and family, as well as riding with various biker clubs without a worry in the world. At one point while in Los Angeles, Beverly and Bernard had no job, money, place to live, or food to eat. Even worse, was that Beverly was pregnant with their first son. After three months of living on the street, lying, cheating, and stealing to feed themselves, Beverly called her mother and asked for permission to return home. Her mother wired her money for a bus ride home on the same day. Beverly left Bernard in Los Angeles and returned to her parent's home.

At the age of 20, with a newborn baby, Beverly quickly became bored while watching her young sister, cousins, and friends having fun attending high school ball games, along with having the freedom to come and go without the headaches of raising a baby. By this time, she had a 10-week-old son. Beverly yearned to see Bernard again because he was someone who loved her and she recalled having daily fun with him. She quickly forgot about living on the streets of Los Angeles.

Snapping out of her daydream, Beverly noticed that the person outside parking the motorcycle was a woman. She smiled. The biker stepped off the bike and removed her left glove from her hand. Beverly saw that the biker was a black female; she smiled again and slowly admired the perfect shape of the biker's body. As she sat at the Starbucks table, she continued to marvel at the biker's every movement. The lady removed the second glove from her hand and placed it on her seat. Beverly was in awe of how well kept her hands were - fingernails nicely polished with a mature and conservative look. She was in love with the biker because she was everything she wanted for herself.

Slowly removing her helmet, the biker placed it on top of her gloves and then used her fingers to comb out her hair. Beverly was really impressed with the tall, sexy, black female biker with long hair, a perfect body, black leather attire, and two-inch heeled boots. The woman turned around and quickly made eye contact with Beverly. Instantly, Beverly's heart dropped, as she was looking eye-to-eye with Joanne Sharanay McCoy, who was First Lady of Abundant Truth Baptist Church.

Joanne unzipped her leather jacket and walked toward the entrance of Starbucks. She entered the coffee shop, proceeded to the counter, and purchased a bottle of water. She handed the young lady behind the counter two, one-dollar bills then walked over to join Beverly Lots in the corner.

"What are you doing here?" Beverly asked Joanne with a mean expression on her face.

"I'm here to see you. You did tell me you would be here," Joanne replied with a smile and then opened her bottled water, took a sip, and placed it on the table.

"Yes, but why are we meeting?"

"Well I was at the hair salon and..." Before Joanne could say another word, Beverly interrupted.

"Listen here lady; I know you're here to talk about the statement I made at the last church meeting. And trust me, no matter what you or your husband say, things are not going to change. The Culinary Ministry is my ministry and I will run things based on my experience and what I think is right. That's what I said to your husband, Pastor Jerome Samiah

McCoy, as well as the entire church. If the church board doesn't like the way I'm running my ministry, they can replace me. I take my orders from the most high, my Lord and Savior, Jesus Christ."

"In all honesty, I really don't care what you and the pastor thinks. If the congregation doesn't like the food I provide, tell them not to eat it. I cannot believe the pastor has the audacity to say I need to provide a healthy menu options for the members. Each Sunday, people eat what I provide them; and trust me when I say that every Sunday, the food is all gone. So why should the church spend money trying to feed people healthy food if they're not complaining?"

"The problem is not the food I'm putting out; the problem is people are lazy. Young kids today sit around their homes, play video games, and surf the Internet all day. Some of the local high schools only have a varsity team for sports. They should have a freshman and sophomore team as well. The reason they only have a varsity team is because these young children today don't want to play sports. Also, their stupid parents allow them to lounge about and be lazy. It would be okay if they stayed home and read some books instead of constantly using cell phones, Internet, TV, and video games."

"Tell the pastor to preach to the parents about being good parents. Tell him to talk to the young kids about exercising and not being so lazy. Tell him to organize an exercise club. He looks like he works out daily. Last, tell him to stay out of my ministry. I was running it before he arrived and I believe I'll be running it long after he's gone, I promise you that!" Taking a sip of her caramel flan latte with whipped cream, Beverly smiled.

Joanne smiled also, took a drink from her water bottle and then smiled again. It was the most beautiful smile a person could have.

"Ms. Lot, please accept my apology if I misled you. I'm not here to talk about church business. We can do that during the church business meeting. Also, the pastor is capable of speaking for himself; he doesn't need me to speak on his behalf."

"As I was saying, I was at the hair salon at River City Marketplace for the past three weeks helping Demetrius, my hairstylist, open his new salon. Demetrius and one of his stylists, Cynthia Brookin, are working hard to open up the salon."

Beverly's heart dropped to her lap, recalling the millions of times when, as a young girl, her would tell her and her sister to always be mindful of the things you do and say, because what you do in the dark will come to light. She knew one day her past would catch up with her; she was not thinking it would be today. The name she feared next to Jesus himself was Cynthia Brookin. It sent chills and fear throughout her body as if she was a hyena and Cynthia was Mufasa from the movie *Lion King*.

"Cynthia said she knows you and your husband and have been trying to get in touch with the two of you. I didn't want to give her your phone number without your permission, so she asked me to deliver a package to both of you. She said you guys would be glad to get it." Then Joanne reached into her small, black, Michael Kors bag, pulled out an envelope that was sealed with tape, and handed it to Beverly. Cynthia's name, phone number, email address, and mailing address were on the envelope. Beverly reluctantly accepted the small package. She felt she was being blackmailed, but was not sure what to say.

"I need to go to the restroom; I'll be right back." Joanne excused herself as she rose from her chair and walked to the restroom in the far corner of their location.

Beverly watched Joanne walk away. After she was out of sight, she opened the envelope, and her worst nightmare came true. The past of her and her husband, Deacon Charles Lots, had just caught up with them. She would do anything to keep this information under lock and key. She wondered how much Joanne knew…how much Cynthia shared with her.

At the young age of 20, with a three-month-old son, Bernard returned to Jackson, Mississippi, and reentered Beverly's life. Three months later, Beverly was pregnant and Bernard was locked up for breaking into a local store. After serving one year and a day in the state prison, he was released and resumed his relationship with Beverly once again. She realized her children's father was trouble. Nevertheless, she loved the adventure he brought into her boring life.

At 22-years-old, Beverly was still living with her parents and raising two boys under the age of three. One night, while hanging out with Bernard, he told her he was going to a friend's house. He parked his friend's car on the street, far away from any streetlight, and walked about five houses down. Beverly recognized it was trouble. Therefore, she got out of the car and started walking home. At that point, she knew the relationship between her and Bernard was over. She also had to face the reality that he would not change and she had two sons to raise. Later that night, she learned that Bernard broke into a home, the elderly lady, who was the home owner, died from a heart attack. This time, Bernard was going to prison for murder for 50 years. She was elated she had the strength to get out of the car and walk home that night.

With rumors in the community about her and her boyfriend, the thug, Bernard Williams, Beverly and her mother created a plan for her to move to East St. Louis and stay with her mother's older brother, Pastor Robert Dwayne Bradley. For the next five years of Beverly's life, she went to church and college and focused all of her attention on raising her two sons. When she turned 27, she began dating a church member, Charles Lots, and soon they got married. Her uncle performed the ceremony at his church. Within a year of getting married, Charles' job gave him a promotion and moved the family to Jacksonville, Florida.

This was the third time in Charles's life that he been outside of Illinois – once to Mississippi with Beverly, once on a cruise for his honeymoon, and now Jacksonville. Beverly realized that even with her perfect life, she still had a wild side that kept surfacing. After months of talking to her mother about it, she took her mother's advice and shared her feelings with her husband, hoping he would attend counseling with her.

However, she learned that Charles had a wild side as well. He confessed to his wife about his desires as well as the adventures of his heart. With three children, the two Beverly had prior to meeting Charles and one they had together, the couple decided to act out on their feelings, hoping it was something that would pass soon. Albeit it short, that untamed portion of their lives was a mere figment of their imagination. Regrettably, it was haunting her at the worst time.

Cynthia Brookin was a white female, she was 5'7", a size ten, and loved to wear three-inch heels shoes and short skirts. She was once a principal of a local high school in Jacksonville, Florida. For five consecutive years, she won the Principal of the Year award. However, she was a school principal during the day and an organizer at night, organizing swinging parties between the Jacksonville and Orlando, Florida areas for adult, married couples. After losing her job as school principal due to her late evening entertainment, Cynthia became a hairstylist by day. Yet, she continued to actively arrange adult entertainment–swinging.

Joanne returned from the restroom.

"Well, my work here is done; I need to go now," Joanne announced as she picked up her water and placed it in her Michael Kors bag. "You have a nice day now; I'll see you Sunday in church." Joanne turned around and had taken two steps before Beverly called her name.

"Ms. McCoy, please know I am not one of the women you need to be concerned about."

Beverly was referring to Sofia Gomez and Coleen Walker, two ladies at Abundant Truth Baptist Church, who had the reputation of having love affairs with men of power, such as

CEOs, politicians, as well as leaders and pastors of mega churches. Currently, the two women had Pastor McCoy in their scopes and made it known to many people in the church. Joanne was aware of the females Beverly spoke about. She noticed their aggressive actions within the first month of attending the church.

"Certainly," Joanne replied peacefully with her million-dollar smile as she casually continued to stroll out of Starbucks toward her motorcycle. Beverly sat and continued to glare at Joanne, unsure what to say or do. Reaching into her purse, Beverly removed her cell phone, got up from her table, and started walking toward her car.

"We need to talk. Where are you?" Beverly asked her husband, Charles.

"I'm home cleaning the garage. You okay dear?" Charles inquired.

"Yes, I'm well but we need to talk. I'll be home in about 15 minutes."

"Okay, I'm here."

Beverly positioned herself comfortably behind the steering wheel of her Lexus and started driving.

****

Joanne arrived at her home located on Lancashire, parked her motorcycle in the garage, and walked into the house. Then she entered her husband's office where he was preparing himself for Sunday. Jerome turned his chair around to receive his wife as she walked into his office, and then sat on his right leg in his lap. Jerome slowly caressed Joanne's perfectly shaped onion as she placed her hands around his neck. They both gave each other a big kiss as if they had not seen one another in months.

Pastor Doctor Jerome Samiah McCoy is thirty-five years old and experiencing all the challenges of a new pastor that he learned about when he studied at the University of

Washington and Seattle University, as well as a pastor in training in the local church he grew up in. While in high school, Jerome played sports year round; football, basketball and baseball. Although he finished high school at the bottom 10% of his graduation class, he was offered various sports scholarship for the various sports he played in high school and so he attended the University of Washington on a baseball scholarship. After earning his BA degree in Psychology, he worked in the public school system as a school counselor, while he continued his education to becoming a professional Counselor. A few years later Jerome enrolled in Seattle University and earned his Doctoral degree in Pastoral Studies, afterward he was gainfully employed with the college in the School of Theology and Ministry as the Director of Doctor of Ministry Program.

"Baby, how are you today?" Joanne asked her husband, Pastor McCoy.

"I'm well, just polishing up on my sermon for Sunday," he replied.

"What is the message?"

"Am I My Brother's Keeper, from Genesis 4:1-13 with a special focus on verses 9 and 13."

"I'm excited to hear the sermon. You know I always get excited when you're preaching," Joanne said with a bashful smile as she flirted with her husband, referring to being sexually aroused and excited.

"I'm glad you do. I enjoy looking at you as well."

"Have you noticed the ladies in the church watching you while you're preaching?"

"They're not watching me; they're listening to the message."

"Well I'll take care of the roaming eyes. You just keep on preaching."

"I'm surprised you haven't taken care of Sofia and Coleen yet. It's been a few months now."

"I will in time. Since you mentioned them, any texts or pictures from our special friends today?"

For the past few months, Sofia and Coleen had been sending text messages to Jerome via his cell phone, as well as sending pictures and leaving messages for him in his office. They never attached their names to their text messages and when they sent pictures, their faces were not visible in them. Jerome had never responded to any of the messages.

"A few from last night and today." Jerome reached behind him to his desk where his cell phone was located, picked it up and handed it to Joanne. Joanne read the messages and viewed the pictures.

"They're getting more assertive."

"Why do you say that?"

"They're sending pictures in their undies now. Wow!"

"So when do we put an end to all of this?"

"When they add their face or names to their handiwork, meanwhile we just ignore them."

"Really babe! Are you for real?"

"Yes, trust me, and when they do, I will definitely end all of it."

"I know you will babe, that's why I love you so much."

"I wish you would find time to ride with me. I really miss us riding on the weekends."

"Your hair looks nice. How was your day?" Jerome was changing the subject and Joanne knew it.

"Thank you. Demetrius did it. His new salon is looking really nice. I think it's in a very good location for business," Joanne replied with a smile, realizing her husband was avoiding her question.

"Good, but you've been gone for quite a while. Is everything okay?"

"Yes, I made a stop for coffee. How do you feel about going out for dinner?"

"Coffee? I didn't know you drank coffee."

"It was business. It wasn't good, but good will come from it."

"What?"

"Anyway, what do you say about going out tonight for dinner?"

"Not a problem. I did season your steak, but we can have it for dinner tomorrow if you like," said Jerome.

"If you're cooking, we can stay in. I'm going to change. Do you need help?" Joanne asked as she exited her husband's home office and walked down the hall to her reading room. Joanne entered the room, unlocked the large, mahogany chest, removed an envelope from her MK bag, and placed it in the chest. Then she went into her bedroom and changed clothes. After getting in some comfortable clothes Joanne stretched out across their king size bed with her cell phone and called her mentor, role model, best friend and her mother, Valerie. Valerie is always glad to hear from her baby girl. This is the first time her daughter been so far away from home, a place where they had no friends or family support. And to add salt to an open wound Jerome was in a new position and facing more than the normal challenges of being a first time pastor. Although Joanne's parents tried talking the couple out of moving almost three thousand miles across the country, Jerome made matter worse by asking everyone not to visit them for the first year.

Jerome was offered several dozen pastoral positions within a few hundred miles from home, he ignored the advise from his in-laws to stay close to home and followed the advise of his pastor and many of the older man in his local church in

Washington; such as move your wife away from home so the two of you can depend, support, and grown on each other, and trust in the Lord Jesus to increase and lead you as a new pastor. Although Jerome's pastor and the other men in the church were referring to a few hundred miles from home, they were not talking about from the West coast to the east coast, but they were too head strong to correct themselves after hearing that he accepted a position from the church that is the furthers from home.

Valerie loved Jerome, she watched him grew up since his first birthday. For many years she viewed Jerome and his father as a curious couple, from the first day they moved in the vacated house next door to them. But as the years passed she allowed her curiosity to go and her love for the two of them increased daily. Since Jerome was a young boy in middle school, she always hoped her daughter, Joanne, would become a couple with Jerome.

"Mom," Joanne said with tears in her eyes

"Yes Baby, how are you today?"

"I am well, I am well mother."

"But you are crying, why?"

"The people mother, it hurts how the people treats Jerome. He tries so hard, and the people are so mean."

"He is smart, and he is about the Lord's work, be patient, all will be OK. So, how is the First lady?"

"The First Lady," Joanne replied with a smile and tears. "It's not what I thought it would be as the pastor's wife."

"And you remember what I told you?"

"Yes, I know mom, stay strong, support the pastor, pray, stay positive, always smile and never let them see your weakness."

"I know it's hard, but stay strong and in prayer."

Joanne and her mother continued to talk for the next hour, as they do each day.

****

Beverly arrived home in Simonds-Johnson Park. Although she and her husband could afford to live in a more expensive neighborhood, they had personal reasons for why they lived in that community instead. Beverly spotted her husband outside. As she walked toward him, he detected an unpleasant expression on her face. Beverly handed him an envelope; the same one Joanne handed her in Starbucks. Then she kissed him and entered their house. Charles followed his wife inside, and then removed the items from the envelope. The couple walked to the dinner table and sat down. Beverly watched her husband as he examined the items.

The pictures Cynthia sent them were of their one and only time attending one of Cynthia's adult-married couple swinging parties.

"Who gave you these?"

"Joanne."

"Who?"

"Joanne McCoy."

"The First Lady of the church?"

"Yes!"

"How did she get these pictures?"

"Cynthia."

"How do they know each other? Is she part of Cynthia's circle? Do the first lady and pastor swing?" Charles asked emotionally.

"All I know is Joanne met Cynthia while helping a mutual friend, Demetrius, open a new hair salon."

Charles and Beverly just looked at each other, confused as to what to say or do. What they thought was behind them, they were now facing. How to handle it was even more of a mystery.

"So did she hand the envelope to you like this–open?"

"No, it was closed and sealed."

"You think she knows what's in it?"

"Though she didn't show any signs of knowing, I'm sure she does. I can feel it, every fiber of my body tells me she knows."

"So what do we do?"

"It is blackmail."

"Did she ask for anything?"

"She wants me to give into the pastor's demands and support his goal and vision by providing more healthy food to the members."

"That's what she asked for?"

"No, but there's no other reason for her to be playing such games."

"Is it possible that she was only a messenger for Cynthia, and has no clue to what was in the envelope?"

"She was aware that the message could have waited until Sunday or the next time we saw each other. But a blackmailer goes out of their way to set up a special meeting. They want to see how you respond when the information is delivered."

"Really, how do you know so much?"

"What was my Bachelor and Master degree in, and what do I do for a living?"

"Okay, maybe you're correct, but she didn't ask for anything?"

"Nothing!"

"So what do we do?"

"I'm going to BJ's. I need to buy some healthy food for the church," Beverly replied.

Charles made his point. "Since the pastor started talking about changing the food at the church, you have made it known to the devil himself, you would not be changing your menu. Suddenly, after one meeting with the First Lady, you're modifying meals. I tell you this. If you start making alterations to the menu and she'll keep pulling your strings and controlling you. Do not go down that road with her or you'll never be free of it."

"And if you're wrong, you better be ready for this information to be exposed to all social media outlets, friends, and family."

"Babe, we're children of the Lord Jesus. We're born again; we shouldn't have these fears and concerns."

"I agree, but do you want this information out?" Beverly responded firmly.

"I don't want that to happen but…"

"Charles! We have children in college. There's also the community, friends, our jobs, and church family. This will at least buy us some time until we can decide what to do."

"Though I hate it, you're right."

"It's only fruit, turkey meat, and no pork. I'm only serving healthy food for the members." Beverly said with a smile on her face. Beverly stood up, walked out of her house, got into her car then headed to BJ's.

****

"…and Cain had the audacity to say to God, 'My punishment is greater than I can bear.' Cain was a murderer, a killer, the first recorded killer known to mankind. He killed his brother; his only concern was himself. Did he give his brother Abe an option? Did his baby brother have a chance to say it's more than I can bear? No!" Pastor McCoy delivered his sermon, using his loud voice as he preached during the morning church service.

"Look at all of those ladies sitting up front. Not one has a pen or paper taking notes. Instead, they're all looking at the pastor, wishing he were going home with them. They should be ashamed of themselves," said Anthony Smith to Jean Louis. They were the two male ushers standing at the double doors opposite the pulpit.

"That's cold man. You shouldn't think like that."

"It's true. Just look at them. They all want him."

"Not all. My wife is going home with me, trust me on that."

Anthony Smith was a single man, never been married, but had three children from three different ladies. None of his children or his children's mother attends Abundant Baptist. He was 6'3" and was once a local basketball star in high school with expectations to play professional. On the day he graduated from high school, he was drinking and driving and hit a judge. No one was hurt, but after the media report on his drinking and driving, his scholarship was taken away from him and he spent the last ten years of his life racking himself. He started attending church after befriending Jean Louis, a co-worker at Naval Station Mayport. Jean Louis was born and raised in Abundant Baptist Truth Baptist Church; his grandfather once was the pastor of the church. He is the fourth generation of his family to attend the church and him and his wife; as well as their parents are very active members of the church. Jean attended and played football for Florida State. He was 6'2", weighed 280 pounds of solid muscle, with a bald head and a mustache. While in college he pledged Omega Psi Phi and has the fraternity's brand on his chest and biceps and his wife attended the same college and was a member of the Delta sorority.

"Preach pastor!," Yelled one of the women in the congregation.

"Am I my brother's keeper? Is not the older supposed to provide and protect the younger? Cain's only concern was Cain. Check this out. Cain said to the LORD, my punishment is too great to bear! All Cain cared about was himself. There was no fear or reverence for God, no regret for the loss of innocent life, no sorrow for sin, and no thought for his parents who had lost one son tragically through murder and would be losing another through exile. He was excessively selfish. Cain, the killer, the murderer, greatest fear was being killed."

The pastor finished his message for the morning and closed out the 8:00 a.m. service. Typically, the pastor didn't preach the morning service. It's usually the time for pastors in training to preach. However, the person scheduled to preach was not in service, so the pastor took the pulpit. It was 9:10 a.m. Sunday school classes typically began at 10:00 a.m. and noonday service at 11:30 a.m. Breakfast at the church was served between 9:00 and 10:00 a.m. As the pastor concluded the 8:00 a.m. service, he blessed the food in the dining area for breakfast then returned to his office to rest prior to the noon service.

Everyone in the congregation slowly walked into the dining area for breakfast. One by one, each person was astonished by what they saw. The tables were covered with special cloth table covers. Each table was adorned with fresh flowers. The coffee area had two different types of liquid cream instead of the standard powered stuff that was usually placed on tables. There were stir sticks, not plastic knives, and a variety of teas. In addition to sugar on the table, there were three types of sugar substitutes–Sweet 'N Low, Splenda, and Equal. There was a fruit area, which never existed at the church for breakfast or any other meal. It included items such as watermelon, grapes, grapefruits, apples, oranges, and bananas. In addition to the fruit area, there was a cold cereal station; as well as a section with wheat bread and an assortment of bagels. Finally, there was turkey sausage and turkey bacon. Beverly Lots was there to welcome her church family into the dining area.

Kalevi Dameon Richardson was a local homeless man who attended church service and Sunday school every Sunday along with Wednesday night Bible study. Everyone in the church and community knew him. Sadly, only Joanne showed him respect and love. Many people avoided him due to his dirty look and the stench from his body and clothes. Nonetheless, Kalevi was very respectful of everyone inside and outside the church. Currently, he lived in one of the abandoned buildings next to the church. Prepared to speak to her, Kalevi approached Joanne. She was the only person in the church who talked to him and treated him as if she didn't notice his unsanitary appearance and nose-assaulting aroma.

"Good morning, Ms. First Lady." Kalevi greeted as he reached out to hug and kiss Joanne on the chin.

"Kalevi, how are you today?"

"I'm good. Will you have any work for me this week?" Since Joanne had been attending Abundant Truth Baptist Church, she had been helping Kalevi and other homeless in the community to find construction work within the neighborhood. In some cases, she had been paying them out of her own money.

"Yes, call me in the morning. There's some construction work taking place not too far from here. The foreman will pay you daily, but he really prefers to pay once a week. We can talk in the morning."

"What about my friends?" Kalevi looked out for his other homeless friends. There were four of them who lived in the same abandoned building as Kalevi. However, he was the only one to attend the church regularly.

"We'll see," Joanne replied.

****

"Good morning everyone, I know you're surprised, but this is the new and healthy breakfast food. The pastor said we should eat healthy. Therefore, at Abundant Truth Baptist Church, you will receive healthy food choices. Please come in and relax."

Charles walked up to his wife and whispered in her ear, "Do you think you're taking it too far?"

"I love you as well baby," said Beverly as she gave him a kiss and walked on.

Knowing full well how Beverly felt about changing the breakfast menu, people were shocked at what they were seeing and hearing.

"What happened to your wife, Charles?" One of the deacons in the church asked.

"She's supporting the pastor's vision which we all should be doing." Charles responded then walked away as the deacon looked on in shock.

Beverly walked up to Sister Charlene Monk, who was head of the Health Ministry.

"Charlene, good morning; I was hoping we could work together in promoting healthy eating. I think it would be good if we could hold some workshops and provide information to the members."

"Are you working for the pastor now?" Charlene asked.

"What do you mean?"

"You know what I'm talking about."

Beverly saw the first lady walking into the dining area; she needed to talk to her. "Girl, I'll talk to you later," Beverly said to Charlene as she walked away.

"Good morning First Lady. How are you?"

"I'm well. I like the new look; I'm sure the pastor will like it as well. Seems like the people are enjoying it also."

"Good. Just some minor changes to support the pastor's vision."

"What about your budget? Will you be able to sustain this every Sunday?"

"Yes. The table covers are cloth; I'll wash them once a week and dry-clean them once a month. The flowers are coming from my garden; and my neighbor, who works at the local florist, said she would make a donation twice a month. If it costs additional money, I'll treat it as a donation to the church," Beverly conveyed all of this with a smile.

"Do you need me to do anything?"

"No! No additional help from you is needed. You've done enough."

"Really?"

"Really. Just relax and know the Culinary Ministry is 100% behind the pastor's vision. Whatever he needs, tell him to ask. We're onboard."

"Thank you!," the First Lady stated as she walked away. Beverly continued walking around, talking to various members of the church.

"Sunday school will be starting soon and everyone has a class to attend," Beverly announced as she strolled around the dining area.

Sofia Gomez was an attractive Latino. She was 31 years old; a graduate of Concorde Career College School of Nursing and had self-appointed herself as Pastor McCoy's personal nurse. She also handled his dry cleaning and cleaned his office. Many of her friends had told her she looked like Eva Mendes. Sofia was in the pastor's office; she provided him a bottle of water out of his small, office size refrigerator then proceeded to restock it with water and juice.

Coleen was an attractive, black female. She was also 31 years old and a graduate of Concorde Career College. Every

Sunday, Coleen made it her personal business to bring the pastor breakfast, which included coffee or tea and a bowl of fruit.

As Coleen was heading toward the pastor's office, Sofia, who was behind the door, noticed Coleen walking into the pastor's office. As soon as Coleen entered the doorway, Sofia pushed the door closed as if she didn't see Coleen. The door slammed into the tray Coleen was carrying, causing the hot coffee to spill all over Coleen's clothes. Sofia acted as if it was an accident, but Coleen recognized it was done purposely. Seconds later, Joanne arrived. Noticing the mess, she witnessed Sofia and Coleen apologizing to each other and cleaning up the spill.

"What a mess ladies," Joanne acknowledged as she entered the pastor's office and closed the door. "They're getting more bold," Joanne told her husband. Pastor McCoy shook his head as if he couldn't believe what was happening.

Chapter Two
The Health Ministry

Joanne was at Bailey's Health and Fitness Center. She had just finished a forty-five minute workout on the elliptical machine. As soon as she stepped off the machine, she stepped directly into the path of Charlene Monk.

Charlene was 5'5" 120 pounds with no fat, with short hair that was twisted. She was known as a being a health junky. She was cautious about the food she ate and beverages she drank, she exercised four to six days a week and only ate organic food. She had a short list of friends because she was always counseling friends and family on what they are eating and how they should exercise more.

"Charlene...good afternoon. How are you today?" Joanne asked.

"I'm well, Joanne. It's nice to see you here. I didn't know you were a member of this fitness center?"

"I'm not. This is my first time here. I used one of those fliers that you placed in the church vestibule. You know the one that said your first visit was free."

"Good, I didn't know the members were using them."

"Well just between you and me, I have three," Joanne disclosed with a smile.

"So what's next for your workout?"

"I'm going to try the fruit bar, relax, then a one hour walk on the treadmill," Joanne replied.

"I was heading in that direction myself. May I join you?"

"You promise not to talk about church business?" Joanne smiled.

"Not me."

"Good. Let's go girl."

Charlene and many others at the church viewed the pastor and his wife as a mystery. Charlene had a PhD in Psychology and believed she was more than qualified to get information out of Joanne McCoy, the First Lady. They walked over to the food stand and prepared a small plate full of fruit and then took a seat at the bar.

"Joanne, I know the pastor wants the Health Ministry to organize workshops on healthy eating and living, promote exercising within the church and community, and try to get some of the fitness centers in the city to give promotional memberships to some of the underprivileged members of the church and community. I also know he wants the health and culinary ministries working as a team to encourage good eating and living, as well as having theme months such as, breast cancer, diabetes, prostate cancer, etc. and organize some 3K, 5K, and 9K walk/run event dates. But I just don't think all of that is necessary. People don't need a fitness center to exercise and they can Google information on the Internet about healthy eating and diabetes."

"No church business, remember?" Joanne chided with a smile as she ate her fruit.

"Please accept my apology, but it was on my mind and I needed to get it out. The Health Ministry is mine. I understand the pastor said it's a vision the Lord gave him, but the Lord speaks to me as well and he's not telling me to do those things." Grinning, Charlene looked at Joanne as she asked, "You know what I mean?"

Joanne smiled at Charlene and repeated, "Remember, no church business today."

Charlene quickly realized she was unable to lure Joanne into her conversation. Nevertheless, she was determined to gain some insight about her pastor and first lady. Therefore, Charlene changed her approach and readdressed Joanne.

"So how are you fitting into Jacksonville?" Charlene asked.

"We love the Sunshine State."

"Good. How long has it been now?"

"Three, maybe four months. I think in a week or two it will be four months."

"Is it everything you two thought it would be? Were you looking for a bigger, more up-to-date church in a better neighborhood?"

"The church is exactly what we assumed it would be. We're very happy."

Charlene was shocked by Joanne's statement. She assumed the area–the inner city and the people - all blacks, would have certainly surprised the white pastor.

"That's good to know. I was not on the board for selecting the new pastor, but we all received one vote. The selection process lasted more than a year. In the interim, we had all types of people coming to the church to preach."

"We were slightly surprised that we didn't get an invite to come to the church."

"I was told that the church couldn't afford to fly the two of you out for the weekend, so we settled for the videos."

"Did you actually watch the videos?"

Charlene was tired of the small talk. She was ready to get to what she and many others wanted to know.

"So how did you two meet?"

"We grew up next to each other; we went to the same church, elementary, middle, and high school, and then the same college."

Charlene assumed Joanne only had a high school education and a certificate from one of Seattle's local cosmetology schools. She was so concerned about getting dirt on the pastor and first lady; she missed it when Joanne said she and the pastor went to the same college.

"That's Seattle, Washington, correct?"

"Well South Seattle, the Rainier Beach community. Do you know the area?"

"No, never been there."

"And you, born and raised?" Joanne inquired.

"Born in Benton, Arkansas just south of Little Rock. After high school, I went to Atlanta, Georgia for college - Spelman. There, I met Richard. He's a Morehouse graduate. After college, we worked in the local area for a year then returned to college–University of Georgia for our PhDs. We moved out west – Pasadena, California for about 10 years then moved to Florida about six years ago and have been here since then."

"Pasadena?" Joanne asked as she shook her head, rolling her lips into her mouth as if she was trying to recall something from her memory. "Do you know an Arthur Brown – Arthur Jason Brown, nickname AB?"

Charlene choked up. She knew Arthur Brown much too well. Joanne knowing him as well was not a good thing. In Jacksonville, Florida, only she and her husband, Richard should know about him. Charlene was losing at her own game. However, she refused to give up, and she refused to lose. She still thought she could outsmart Joanne anytime, anyplace, and on any topic. Smiling, she continued to talk, not comprehending that silence was golden to the foolish.

"How do you know Arthur Brown?"

"He's my brother-in-law. He used to be a parole officer in Pasadena about the same time you lived there; now he's the DA. When I told him we were moving out here, and about the church, he mentioned your name. As soon as you mentioned Pasadena, California, it all came back to me."

"Your brother-in-law, the DA," Charlene reaffirmed. Now Charlene believed Joanne knew about her family and why they moved from California to Florida. "One would have never thought," Charlene responded.

Smiling, Joanne said, "Do you think you and your family will ever move back to Pasadena?"

Charlene knew the answer was no; they could never move back to Pasadena. Now Charlene wanted to know how much Joanne knew about her family. Conversely, the more she talked, the deeper the hole she was digging herself into. Finally, she decided to remain quiet. She also believed the two of them meeting today was not accidental; it was planned by Joanne. Charlene's phone rang.

When Charlene and her family were living in Pasadena, California, her twin sons, who were 12 years old at the time, were charged with raping boys and girls at their middle school. With the support of a State Senator, Charlene and her husband were able to make arrangements with Arthur Brown to move out of the state so their sons could get a new start in life. The boys attended counseling until their 21st birthday and reported to the DA office in Pasadena monthly.

"Excuse me. I need to take this," Charlene communicated as she walked away from Joanne.

"Hello babe, how are you?" Charlene greeted the person on the phone and then looked back at Joanne and whispered to her, "It's Richard."

"Babe, I called to see what you would like to do for dinner tonight. It is Wednesday, Bible study night."

"Babe, we have a problem, a serious problem on our hands."

"Like what?"

"Arthur Brown is the brother-in-law of Joanne McCoy."

"So what's the problem?"

"She knows about our past."

"What makes you think that?"

"Trust me, she knows. I can read it all over her face."

"Come home and we can talk about this."

"Bye."

"Bye."

Charlene hung up the phone and walked toward Joanne.

"I need to go. I'll see you tonight at Bible study," Charlene informed Joanne as she walked toward the doors that led outside. Joanne continued eating her fruit, as if she was having a great and productive day.

****

Charlene arrived home, parked her car, and walked into the house. Her husband, Richard, was sitting on the patio deck. She got a cold drink from the kitchen fridge, slid the patio door open, walked onto the patio, and then sat next to her husband.

"Babe, what's the problem? What makes you think our family secret has been exposed?" Richard asked his wife.

"I can just tell. She waited for the special moment then asked me did I know Arthur Brown, who is her brother-in-law and now the DA in Pasadena."

"How did you two get on the subject?"

"We were just talking and it came up."

"Did it simply come up, or were you probing for answers and she reversed your game on you?"

Charlene turned her face and looked in the opposite direction and then back to her husband.

"Whatever happened, the bottom line is she knows."

"Did she say anything directly related to us, or is it just because she knows Arthur?"

"Richard, she knows about us and she knows our family secret. What happened in Pasadena has finally caught up with us in Florida."

"Arthur cannot talk about his cases. By law, he cannot reveal that information to anyone, not even the woman in his bed."

"We can fix it. We're not exposed to the social medias of the world. We'll be okay."

"You're confusing me."

"The first lady is blackmailing me to do what the pastor wants me to do in the Health Ministry. I'll give in so that she doesn't expose our family secret, trust me."

"How do you assume that?"

"Trust me, please baby trust me. I can fix this. We'll be okay."

"Babe, let's pray and ask Jesus for direction."

"Later, I have some important work to do now. I need to fix things."

"Okay, we'll do it your way, but as soon as I feel things are getting out of control, I'm stepping in and taking charge of things. You hear me!"

"Yes, but it'll be okay, trust me," Charlene declared as she stood up.

"Where are you going now?" Richard asked.

"I need to get ready for Bible study."

"What about dinner, babe?"

"Please order pizza. I have a few announcements to get ready for," Charlene informed her husband as she kissed him and walked away.

****

"I can do all things in Christ who strengthens me. Paul has experienced various circumstances. In Philippians 4:13, he comes to the conclusion that he could conquer all things such as, any trial, burden, or evil. Various changes in Paul's life warranted him to arrive to that conclusion. Paul now expresses the firm confidence that nothing would be required of him he would not be able to perform," Pastor McCoy lectured.

It was Wednesday night Bible study at Abundant Truth Baptist Church; the lesson was having strength in Jesus Christ.

"Do you think he believes all the stuff he's saying?" Adam Troy asked Eric Beam. They were two, adult, male members in the church who were in their late thirties.

"Brother, you will have to ask him that," replied Eric.

"Do you believe all of that?"

"Are you listening to the teaching? Paul's life experience got him to that belief system. Paul was not born thinking and saying that."

"I know, but you know what I mean? To say you can do all things is a big statement; do you think the pastor believes that stuff?"

"Yes, I think he believes what he's saying. His teaching is deep. The man knows the bible."

"Well if he believes what he's saying, he should be at a mega church outside of the city. You know the only people that pastor small, inner city churches are the new ones and the ones that can't preach or teach – you know, the low paying ones."

"Dude, you really need Jesus. You have some issues."

"It's true."

"Whatever."

"...Paul's life experience had brought him to the mature level to say, 'Through Christ who hath strengthened me, I can do all things.' It was not in any natural ability that he had; not in any vigor of body or of mind; not in any power which were of his own resolutions; it was in the strength he derived from the Redeemer. By that, he was enabled to bear cold weather, fatigue, and hunger; by that, he met temptations and persecutions; and by that, he engaged in the performance of his arduous duties. We are not to dread what is to come. Trials, temptations, poverty, want, and persecution may await us; but we need not sink into despondency. At every step of life, Christ is able to strengthen us, and can bring us triumphantly through. That's my time. We've come to the end of our lesson. Are there any announcements before closing out Bible study?"

Charlene Monk raised her hand.

"Pastor, I have a few announcements...if I can, please."

"Sister Monk, please feel free to speak."

"My church family, I want to make a quick announcement about the changes that will be taking place within the Health Ministry. Starting tomorrow, there will be a monthly theme. Each month, we will have specific teachings regarding topics related to healthy living, such as, breast cancer, diabetes, heart disease, high blood pressure, and high cholesterol. I think you all get the picture. I will be asking for volunteers to sponsor three or four walking and running marathons for the remainder of the year. Also, I will be working with Sister Lots in sponsoring a few workshops on healthy eating and living."

Beverly Lots looked at Charlene Monk, wondering what happened to her. Then she quickly realized what forced her to change her thought process as well as changes to her ministry.

Charlene continued with, "And you all know there are seven, Bailey's Health and Fitness Centers within the city limits of Jacksonville. Well each center is going to give one free membership for the year to a member of the church. I will consult with the pastor to see how those seven will be selected. That's all for now. More information will follow."

Everyone in the church applauded.

"What happened to your wife? What she said today is a big change from her stance two weeks ago," said Deacon Otis Danish to Charlene's husband, Richard. Richard merely smiled and clapped his hands.

"Sister Monk, please get with the Multimedia Ministry and place some information on the church's website."

"Sure Pastor, whatever you say," Charlene replied with a smile.

"Does anyone else have an announcement before praying and departing for the evening?"

The pastor closed out Wednesday night Bible study with a prayer and then everyone slowly left the church. Kalevi walked up to the first lady for a conversion.

"Ms. First Lady, thank you for the work; my friends thank you as well. The foreman said he has work for us for the next three months and maybe longer."

"You're welcome Kalevi. How are your friends?"

"We all are well. I'll make sure they all come to church soon. They feel ashamed about not having decent clothes to wear. Do you think you can help?"

"Not a problem. I'll get back to you; have a nice day."

Joanne went to her husband's office and together they exited the church and drove home.

****

"I think that was nice of Sister Monk. What do you think?" Joanne asked her husband as they navigated the city streets of Jacksonville, Florida.

"Yes, surprising, but very nice."

"Babe, what's bothering you?"

"All is well, baby."

"Tell me. I know something deep is on your mind."

"The people here hate me. I feel like I'm forcing myself on them. Do you think we should leave?"

"They selected you as the pastor; you are the pastor. Accept it and embrace your role." Joanne loved her husband and gave him the utmost respect but she recalled the days of her youth as a high school student and skipping classes. Her father came to her high school and met her in the school cafeteria when she was scheduled to be in class. He chastised her in front of her classmates and school staffers – everyone in the cafeteria. In school, Joanne cried for the rest of the day and was teased by many of her peers. After school, her father took her out for a one-on-one and taught her true love sometimes means tough talk.

"Well something is strange, it's not just the people in the church, but people outside the church as well. It seems like no matter what I try to do, there are roadblocks. Someone is always giving me a hard time."

"Babe, they're not fighting you; they're fighting against Christ. Again, if it was easy, anyone could pastor the church. As you have reminded me for years, life doesn't get easy when you're working for Jesus. The closer we get to Him, the harder Satan works on us. For that reason, if Satan is working on you, you must be getting extremely close to Jesus."

"Thanks babe, what will I do with you?"

"You want to know?"

"Not now; I love you," Pastor McCoy replied with a smile.

"So when do we christen your office?" Joanne teased, displaying a bashful smile.

"We already did and more than once. We can do it again tonight if you like."

"I was talking about your office at church."

"You're a crazy woman. You cannot be for real," Jerome beamed.

Joanne grinned; her husband was well aware that she was dead serious.

"Just say when, I do have the keys."

"I'm thinking between services on Sunday."

"No way! What if someone walks in?"

"It's your office. Lock the door, Pastor McCoy."

****

"Babe, I think tonight is a good night for a family trip to DQ," Charlene told Richard.

"Cool. Tell me, do you think you laid it on a little thick tonight?" Richard asked Charlene.

"No, it was just right. I'm sure we won't have a problem with her."

"I think you should have taken baby steps, a little at a time. It would be nice to know if she knows anything."

"Let's leave it alone. Please don't say anything to her, please."

"Only if you make the same promise, dear," Richard countered.

"That's a promise. I don't care to speak to that woman again," Charlene avowed, even though she didn't mean what she was saying. She had already started thinking of a way to get the upper hand on Joanne Sharanay McCoy.

As far as Charlene was concerned, Joanne was a graduate from a local cosmetology school in the Seattle, Washington area and lacked the intelligence to match her and her BA degree from Spelman as well as her Doctoral degree from the University of Georgia. Based on the fact that her education extended miles beyond hair school, Charlene would learn the hard way that Joanne was too much for her. Furthermore, she was a child of Jesus Christ. Charlene was starting a war she could not win and for which she was not prepared.

****

The house phone rang at the residence of Jerome and Joanne McCoy at 11:45 at night.

"Hello," Joanne answered in a drowsy and sleepy voice.

"Ms. McCoy, may I talk to the pastor? I have a leaking faucet in my bedroom bathroom."

"Who is this?"

"Sister Coleen from the church."

Joanne became angry over the late night phone call. She quickly sits up in her bed and prepared yourself to give Coleen a word-whipping, knowing the woman was after her husband, but she quickly bearded in mind what her mother been teaching her about the characters of The First lady; which were to be peaceful, have a meek and quiet spirit, a servant heart, do not call attention to your physical beauty, always be a joyful person, stay in prayer and remain devoted to God. "Sister Coleen, the pastor knows nothing about repairing a leaking faucet, but I will call Travis and ask him to come over and help you."

"Travis!"

"Yes, he's a very good handyman and will be able to fix your leaking faucet. The pastor is the wrong person to call. I'll call Travis for you."

"Okay, thank you. I have Travis' number; I'll give him a call. You go back to sleep, Ms. First Lady, goodnight." Coleen didn't have Travis' phone number and had been hoping Joanne wouldn't be the one to answer the phone.

"Night," replied Joanne as she disconnected the call.

"Who was that?" Jerome asked.

"One of your floozies has a leaking faucet in her bedroom."

"Bathroom dear," Jerome replied.

"No, her bedroom."

"Okay, good night," he said.

Chapter Three
The Usher

"Calvin!" David Bloat yelled out as he exited his Honda Accord in the church parking lot, and started heading toward the church for their quarterly usher meeting.

"Babe, I'll see you inside the church," Calvin Green said to his wife, Theresa, as he turned around to see why David was yelling his name in the parking lot and running toward him.

Calvin and David were both in their early thirties. Both of them had been members of the church for about three years, and both of them were ushers at the church. Calvin was married with two, young boys and had the desire to be a preacher. David was a single parent of a 12-year-old girl. His daughter's mother was on active duty in the United States Navy station in Kings Bay, Georgia. His daughter visited her mother every weekend and whenever possible. David and Calvin shook hands.

"Good morning, what's going on?" Calvin asked.

"Wednesday night Bible study and all that stuff the pastor said about believing in Christ and you can do all things. Do you believe that stuff?"

"Yes. It's in the Bible and I believe in the bible."

"I think it's misunderstood. Paul was talking about his relationship with Christ, not everyone else."

Calvin smiled, shook his head and asked, "What's your point?"

"Check this out. I have the perfect plan. Last year, Evelyn Harrison mentioned how it would be nice if one of the men in the church could take her son on the Jacksonville Ironman Triathlon."

The Jacksonville Ironman Triathlon is an annual race that consisted of bike riding, jogging, and swimming. Evelyn Harrison's son, Jason Harrison, was 19 years old and had been training to compete in the triathlon since he was 16. When Jason was 17 years old, he received a flu shot. Six days later, he started experiencing a muscle disorder, very similar to Dystonia. Over the next six months, he went from 180 pounds to 95 pounds. Jason talked very little, but his mother had expressed that he still desired to compete in the Triathlon. Unfortunately, his health wouldn't allow him to compete at all. In order for Jason to compete in the race, he would need someone to put him in the wheelchair and push him while they ran then place him in a small boat and pull him while they swam. Finally, it would be necessary to place him on a special made bike for two, while the individual peddled. The race was a total of 72.3 miles, which would begin and end near the Jacksonville Jaguars stadium.

Evelyn was a white female, single, very attractive, and well-educated. When she was 16 years old, she was raped. Her son, Jason, was the result of her rape. At the singles ministry, Evelyn had expressed her desire to meet someone special and get married; every man that looked at her wanted her. No matter where Evelyn was, a man always tried to talk to her. On the other hand, she had not dated seriously in years. She was not convinced that the men she had been meeting could handle a relationship with her son. In addition to the challenges Evelyn had been experiencing with her son and dating, she was also experiencing issues with women hating on her because their husbands couldn't stop looking at and talking about her. This was Evelyn's third church in four years. She had been moving from church-to-church due to the cold reception and hatred of female congregants in the church.

"And?"

"Well let's ask the pastor to take her son; you know the man has been checking her out."

"And how do you know that?"

"Dude, any man that sees that woman wants her. She's fine, educated, has her own money, is nice and polite, and did I say fine?"

"Any man?"

"You know what I mean. Once she and the pastor connect, I'm sure one of them will make a move on the other. Plus, there's no way he'll agree to a race like the Ironman Triathlon. Then all that talk about I can do anything because the Lord has strengthened me, will be proven to be a lie."

"Please stay clear of me because Jesus is going to strike you with lightning."

"Okay, I told you. You'll see."

"David, I've heard the things people have said about the pastor. We spent almost two years, and $50,000 searching for the perfect pastor. We all voted and he's here. The man is a great teacher and preacher. Now because he's not black, we want him to leave. A black pastor was our plan, but we received God's plan for us. Accept it. I like him and his wife; they're good people and truly laboring for the Lord Jesus."

"We'll see," David replied.

The two men walked into the church and proceeded to the classroom where their quarterly usher meeting was being held.

"Good morning saints!" Tyrone Cummings, head of the Usher Ministry, shouted. "First, I want to thank you all for coming to today's meeting. It's 10:00 a.m. now and I assure you all we'll be out of here by noon today. I've purchased some donuts and juices. If you would like some, please do not let Sister Monk or Sister Lots see you eating and drinking them. Soon all sugar products will be banned from the church as we move to a better you through healthy eating and fitness." Tyrone laughed. He was mocking the pastor's theme, which is, "A healthy Christian is a better Christian."

"Now to business. Since our last meeting, I received a few phone calls about why the ushers aren't conducting business in accordance with the pastor's vision. What the pastor wants is less information in the church program on Sundays. He wants us to come out and support other ministries and church events instead of just Sunday services. He wants us to be greeters, smiling and shaking hands with each person that comes into the building. He wants us to escort each person to his or her seat. Finally, he wants us to have three different uniforms: one for a regular Sunday, one for traveling, and one for special events."

"I'm the president of this ministry and here's my take on what the pastor wants. The reason for the church bulletin is to provide and share information between ministries as well as the members of the church. Now the pastor wants to tell each ministry what information they can and cannot share with the congregation. He doesn't have the right to do that."

"There are enough of us to work one service twice a month. If we start supporting other ministries and church events, we'll be at the church three to four times a month and on some Sundays all day. With the price of gasoline, he wants us to do additional traveling. If other ministries need help, they need to recruit more people into their ministry or do less, but leave us alone. Is there anyone here who wants to do more work?" No one in the meeting raised his or her hand. "Just as I figured; we have a good thing going and I'm protecting this ministry."

"Most churches have hospitality and or greeting ministries. If the pastor wants someone smiling and all in people's faces when they walk into the church, he should start another ministry. We're ushers, not the smiling type of people. Besides, the church is not crowded enough to be escorting people to a seat. There's plenty of space. They can find their own place to sit. If they need help, they can ask."

"And finally, why does he want us to purchase additional uniforms? For years before he came, one uniform worked and will continue to do so years after he's gone. It's just a waste of everyone's money. We can find better things to spend money on instead of uniforms to stand around the church opening the door and handing out programs."

"On a different note, this committee has been hurting for years, years, and years before many of you came to this church or joined the Usher Board. The Board of Directors (BOD) asked and appointed me as the president of this ministry. So as far as I'm concerned, any changes need to come from the BOD, not the short-term pastor."

"Brother, I'm a little confused. If we voted for the pastor, and he's the head of the church, why would we not follow his vision?" Calvin Green asked Tyrone.

"It's not that we're not following the pastor's vision. Keep in mind, Jesus speaks to other people as well. So we shouldn't be quick to make changes just because one person thinks it's a good thing. Jesus hasn't given me such a vision. Has anyone else had those visions?"

"Brother Tyrone, I'm simply saying if the pastor is the head of the church, and we voted him as our leader, why are we fighting with him? Roman 13:1 says, "Let everyone be subject to the governing authorities, for there is no authority except that which God has established. The authorities that exist have been established by God."

"Oh, we're throwing scriptures around now? Bring it on."

"Brother, I'm only looking for answers."

"Like doubting Thomas, John 20:25, "Except I shall see in his hands the print of the nails, and put my finger into the print of the nails, and thrust my hand into his side, I will not believe."

"Brother, you taking this the wrong way, it's not doubt."

"What is it then?"

"If we keep reading in Romans, the scripture says when we rebel against authority, we rebel against the Lord."

"Okay, Brother Green, respect this. I am the head authority of this ministry, and I am telling you we are not following the pastor's vision."

"Okay, that's fine with me. I will submit to your authority. I love you, but brother please pray about what you're saying."

"Yeah, I love you too. This meeting is over. Anyone have something to say?"

No one responded.

"Let's get out of here." Tyrone snapped as he angrily walked out of the meeting room and to his car without closing with prayer as usual.

Tyrone was 5' 11", 46 years old, approximately 180 lbs. and dressed and acted as if he were 21 years old. He used lots of street slang when communicating to the youths in the church and the community.

Everyone in the classroom slowly exited as they exchanged words with each other. As Calvin and his wife, Theresa, started to walk out of the church, Calvin noticed David walking from the back of the church toward the pastor and the pulpit.

"Baby, please excuse me. I need to stop this fool from creating additional drama around the church," Calvin explained as he walked away from his wife. He went through a set of doors, leading into the sanctuary and then walked between two of the church pews with the intention of preventing David from talking to the pastor. Regrettably, he didn't make it.

"Pastor McCoy, sir!," Calvin yelled in a somewhat above normal voice. The pastor turned around.

"Brother Calvin, how are you? Are you okay?"

"Yes sir."

"Please wait a minute. Brother David has something to say to me. Yes brother David, what can I do for you today?"

David looked at Calvin who signaled for him to leave without addressing the pastor. At that point, David realized he was in the wrong. Unfortunately, Satan had the best of him now and he was compelled to say what he had to.

"There is a handicapped member of our church who's been crying out for help for a while. I was wondering if you could help the young kid. I'm sure his mother, Sister Harrison, would greatly appreciate it."

Calvin was looking at David; he was extremely angry with him. Calvin immediately interrupted, "Pastor, I'm sure you're too busy right now. What David is referring to requires a person to dedicate approximately eight to ten hours of training daily for about a year and you're too busy for that."

"I'm willing to do what I can to help."

"That's great pastor," said Sofia.

"Good, I'll tell his mother that you'll help him." David replied as he quickly walked off while ignoring the pastor calling his name to come back.

"I got it pastor. I'll talk to David and Jason's mother."

"What is it? What is David talking about? What did I just volunteer for?" Pastor McCoy asked with a silly smile on his face.

"The Jacksonville Ironman Triathlon is a 72.3 mile race in all. It involves jogging, swimming, and bike riding."

Pastor McCoy sat on one of the pews behind him and inhaled deeply. Everyone around was staring at him, wondering if he was okay. Sofia sat next to him, actually very close.

"Pastor, please don't worry about this. I can handle it."

"Explain to me how Jason, being handicapped, is supposed to do a 72.3 mile race, and how am I to help?"

Calvin looked around at everyone. He was angry with David, but he was gone. David had done the work of Satan and left.

"Pastor, Jason is about 95 pounds and lacks control of his body. You'll have to get one of those jogger wheelchairs and push him while you're running and a special bike for him to ride while you paddle for the both of you. Last, there has to be a rubber boat for him to lie in while you swim and pull him. The total distance is 72.3 miles; the race begins around 6:00 a.m. Normally, the first person wins in roughly nine hours. However, the race ends at midnight, so everyone must be done in 18 hours."

As Pastor McCoy sat on the pew bench smiling, he slowly started shaking his head then stood up.

"Say nothing to Brother David. I'll do the race. I have a meeting to run off to, so please walk with me," Pastor McCoy asked Calvin. As they exited the sanctuary together, Pastor McCoy turned around to talk to Calvin and found Sofia standing there as well. Sister Sofia, please excuse us."

"Yes Pastor, I'll wait for you by your office," Sofia responded as she walked to the Pastor's office. Calvin and Pastor McCoy looked at one another, puzzled as to what she was doing and talking about.

"Brother, I'll need some help, some dedicated men to help me with the race. Can you recruit a few good men, maybe 10 to 12?"

"Pastor, the race is in like six to eight weeks. If you're not ready now, you won't be in eight weeks."

"Get the brothers together please. I need to run. We'll meet soon," Pastor McCoy informed Calvin as he exited the building. Then he got into his Chrysler 300C John Varvatos

Luxury Edition and drove off to a business meeting with city officials.

****

"Kalevi!" Joanne yelled from her car as she saw him standing in the doorway of his abandoned home. Kalevi came out to Joanne's car. She got out and went to her trunk where Kalevi met her.

"Yes, Ms. First Lady?"

"I have some clothing items for you and your friends; I guessed at the sizes, so I hope you all can fit them. I have a meeting I need to run off to now, so we have to chat later. Have a great day!;" Joanne exclaimed while handing a few bags to Kalevi, which were full of clothing, shoes, socks, shirts, and suits.

"Thank you, Ms. First Lady. I'll see you in church on Sunday."

"Bye," Joanne shouted as she got into her car then drove off for a quick trip to Georgia.

****

Tyrone took the Golden Isles Parkway exit, turned right at the end of the ramp and then headed south on Golden Isles Parkway, arriving at the Embassy Suites hotel. He parked his Hyundai Sonata and entered the hotel. Slowly strolling through the hotel lobby, he quickly noticed Joanne McCoy walking with the hotel manager, Cybil Lane.

Joanne approached Tyrone and said, "Mr. Tyrone, I'm surprised to see you here. How are you today?"

Seeing the First Lady of Abundant Truth Baptist Church left Tyrone breathless. He couldn't speak. The cat had truly gotten hold of his tongue. He had just driven 75 miles from home so he wouldn't be seen by anyone he knew in Jacksonville, Florida. Then low and behold, he ran directly into the last person he wanted to see.

"First Lady."

"Mr. Tyrone, this is Cybil Lane. She's the hotel manager; we have a meeting today. Are you okay?"

Before Tyron could say a word, an older man in the doorway of the conference room called out his name.

"Tyrone Cumming, we're waiting on you to get started, come on in please."

Tyrone was bashful. His five-year secret was coming to an end. Right now, he was wondering if Joanne was aware of what was occurring in the conference room and if she would share his dark secret with the congregants, exposing it to everyone in the church, as well as the community.

"Looks like they're waiting on you. I'll see you in the morning at church," Joanne commented as she walked away with Cybil.

Tyrone walked away as well, entered the conference room, and closed the door. For the next two hours, all he could think about was what and how much did the first lady know about him and the meeting he was attending. He also speculated about what she was doing at the hotel in Georgia.

****

It was 6:00 p.m. on a Saturday evening and Pastor McCoy had a full, yet unproductive day of meeting with the church trustees; as well as the city manager and contractors. Consequently, he was enraged. Joanne arrived home after a full day of meetings and was looking for her husband. Hearing her enter their home, Jerome rushed from his home office to the kitchen to meet her.

"Babe, we're leaving this place. I've had enough! I'm announcing our departure tomorrow morning at the morning and noon service!," Jerome expressed angrily. Joanne was in shock at his disclosure.

"I've taken all I'm going to take. They wanted us out of here, so they've won. I can find another church someplace else, but fighting with these people is ridiculous. Not only am I fighting with the church members, now the city officials are opposing me. At today's meeting, the city manager, who is also a member of the church, stated he's never going to issue us a building permit and the trustees looked at him and said okay. The city manager was angry because he allowed the church to build an addition three years ago, but a permit was never applied for. Of all people, the mayor looked at me and said try again next year. Finally, the contractor announced there were rumors that the church doesn't pay its bills. Well it's bull; they just want us out of here and they've won!"

Joanne looked at her husband, put her purse down, and smiled at him. She cautiously selected her words as though she was a sniper waiting for the perfect time to speak.

"Babe, do you remember what you told me when we moved out here?" Joanne inquired in a very nonchalant way.

"What?"

"When we moved out here, what did you tell me, and how did you tell me?" Joanne asked calmly.

"Joanne, just say what's on your mind," Jerome said in an extremely irritated voice.

Taking a deep breath and knowing her mother told her days like this one will come, Joanne said, "Let me remind you. You said something like 'babe, the Lord told me to go to Florida and pastor the church He has set aside for me.' Does that sound about right?"

"Joanne, please say what's on your mind and get it over," Jerome commented, still clearly upset.

Remaining calm, she said, "And you went on to say the Lord spoke to you as if He was speaking to Abram, telling him to leave Uz and go off to a foreign land. Sarai followed

46

her husband, Abram, like a good wife. Do these words sound familiar to you?"

"Well what's your point?"

"My point, Pastor McCoy, is that you and your God had a conversation. You know that I love you and the Lord Jesus, and I'm a believer, but who talked to me? Who asked me about leaving my home and business in South Seattle to go to a foreign place–Jacksonville, Florida–3,000 miles away? No one. Not you, nor your Lord. I simply said okay; I submitted like Sarai. You had your Abram moment and I went along just like Sarai. Now we're here and things aren't going as easy as you would like. There are some challenges in being a pastor. People are fighting against you and you have trials ahead of you. For that, I'm sorry."

Joanne walked up to her husband; they looked at each other face-to-face. With her 5'9" against his 5'11" height, Joanne softly placed the palm of her right hand on Jerome's chest and patted him as if he was a hurt puppy.

"Now babe, please hear me. Just as Jeremiah told the people to get comfortable in Babylon because they were going to be there for a while, you need to get comfortable at Abundant Truth Baptist Church and Jacksonville, Florida. We're not leaving Jacksonville, Florida until I say we're leaving. So you need to go into that room you call an office and sanctuary, and get on your knees and pray because we're going to be here for a while. I know you didn't ask, but I had a very busy day also. I need a hot shower, dinner, and to be held tonight."

Joanne kissed her husband, turned around then walked to her bedroom for a hot shower and a change of clothes. Watching his wife as she walked away, Jerome turned around, walked to his office, and started praying.

****

"Good evening dear. How are you?" Brenda said to her husband, Tyrone. The couple arrived at the same time and stood in the driveway in front of their home.

"I'm well, baby. How was your day?" Tyrone replied.

"From the look of things, better than your day. What's on your mind?"

"Nothing."

"Stop lying and help me with these bags," Brenda retorted. Tyrone followed his wife to the rear of her car, grabbed a few bags from the trunk, and went into the kitchen. Placing three bags of food on the kitchen counter, he returned to the car for the last two bags. Brenda began unpacking the groceries and putting them away just as Tyrone returned with the last two bags of groceries, sat them on the counter, and took a seat at the kitchen table.

"Brenda, please come sit down and talk to me."

Brenda noticed the expression on her husband's face. Slowly, she walked over and took a seat beside him. Tyrone reached out and held her hand.

"While at my AA meeting today, I ran into the First Lady of the church," Tyrone revealed, looking as if he wanted to cry.

Approximately five years ago, Tyrone and Brenda were in Savannah, Georgia, celebrating St. Patrick's Day. Tyrone was drunk and driving back to their hotel located on Abercorn Street. While driving on Montgomery Street, Tyrone stopped at a red traffic light, and a police car stopped behind him. A van full of young, college students, who had been drinking, drove directly into the police car at a speed estimated to be above 50 mph. The force propelled the police car into Tyrone's car, which caused Tyrone to hit several pedestrians crossing the street. Sorrowfully, it resulted in the death of two teenagers. After a long investigation and court trial, Tyrone was not held accountable for the deaths of the teenagers, but was charged with driving while drunk. The judge ordered him to attend AA counseling once a month for eight years. In addition, he had to pay the funeral expenses for both teenagers, but served no time in prison.

No one at the church, his job, or the community was aware of Tyrone's driving incident. He and his wife kept it a secret from many friends and family as well. However, now Tyrone feared that someone in Jacksonville knew; and he wanted to keep that terrible situation in his life a dark secret.

"In Georgia, she was attending the meeting as well?"

"No. She was having some type of meeting with the hotel manager, and as I was approaching the conference room, we ran directly into each other."

"Did you tell her why you were there?"

"No! But Tom was standing in the doorway yelling my name, telling me everyone was waiting on me to get started."

"Did she know what was going on in the conference room? There aren't any signs in the hallway that says AA meeting here, come on in."

"She was walking with the hotel manager. I'm sure the manager gave her the rundown of the whole hotel – for what reason, I have no clue."

"Wow, I find it strange that she was at the hotel and in the area of the conference room at the same time you were scheduled to be there. It's almost like she knew, like she wanted you two to see one another."

"What are you talking about?"

"I wonder if it was deliberate and not coincidental." Brenda pondered aloud.

"Deliberate? How would she know and for what reason?"

"She played you; she just pulled your strings."

"What are you talking about?" Tyrone questioned.

"Think about the last few weeks. Beverly then Charlene and now you. The First Lady of Abundant Truth Baptist Church is a thug and she's going after everyone challenging the pastor's vision and authority."

"You've been known to come up with some extensive conspiracy theories in the past, but this one is deep. You went far out in space for that one. The woman is a hairstylist; her education beyond high school is hair school. She's only been living in the area for a few months. With so little education and the short time she's lived here, not only is she pulling my strings, but two others–no way!"

"Tyrone, that's her secret. She has you people thinking she's a simple, uneducated woman, but she's behind it all. Trust me, her true friends are the ones we church folk, educated, white collar workers ignore; such as the gays and homeless."

"Babe, thank you for your input."

"Low-level workers are attracted to individuals like the first lady because most people assume they're dumb. Therefore, they speak freely around them. You know she hangs out with Demetrius and we know he has the dirt on everyone within 100 miles of Jacksonville."

"Babe...thank you for the education." Tyrone said this in an extremely sarcastic manner.

"Well if you don't believe me, what's your next step? Do you think she'll tell anyone? Do you think your secret for the last few years is still hidden? Are you prepared for this information to be leaked to the church, the community, and your job? Tell me what you're going to do to keep a lid on things?"

Tyrone sat quietly at the table, staring out the patio door into the backyard. Brenda smiled, slowly got up, and returned to unpacking the groceries and putting them away. Five minutes passed with both of them being quiet.

"So let's assume you're right. That the first lady and I meeting at Embassy Suites in Brunswick, Georgia outside the conference room used for AA meetings was not a simple coincidence. What can I do to keep it quiet? What is it that she wants from me? It's not like she and I have been talking."

"She wants the exact something she received from Beverly and Charlene. You expressed quite loudly what you thought about her husband's vision. I told you all that boasting would catch up with you one day. Silence is golden."

"I never disagreed with her husband. I disagreed with the pastor of Abundant Truth Baptist Church. They are two different people and two different issues."

Brenda turned around, faced her husband, placed her hands on her hips, and said, "Really, you think so? Maybe with her simple hair school degree, she can't tell the difference between the man in her bed and the man in the pulpit."

Chapter Four
The Trustee and the City Manager

It was 9:30 a.m. on Sunday morning when Joanne slowly brought her personal vehicle to a complete stop in her reserved parking space at the church. Her father's best friend, Mathew Arden Doorsill, was escorting her.

Mathew Arden Doorsill was born and raised in South Seattle, Washington. He grew up with Joanne's father, Andrew Leroy McKinney. They were like brothers. They both attended the same elementary, middle, and high school. After high school, Mathew went to Bethune-Cookman University on a scholarship to play basketball. He studied law in college and after some years, became a judge in Jacksonville, Florida. Five years ago, he was appointed to the Florida Supreme Court. Currently, his residence was in the Tallahassee, Florida area. He arrived in Jacksonville Saturday evening for a retirement party of a former judge and decided to stay the night to have a late lunch with Joanne and her husband.

Joanne and Andrew walked into the church and then she escorted him to the dining area for a cup of coffee before taking him to the pastor's office. While preparing coffee, Joanne could hear multiple conversations taking place around her and Andrew.

And my job today is to stand in the vestibule or outside by the front door with Sister Troviller and greet people as they enter the church," said an usher to a member of the church.

"I was just getting ready to print the church program when Tyrone called and told me, starting tomorrow, the church program will consist of a single page, folded. Furthermore, per instructions from the pastor, there will be no more 10 to 15 sheets of loose paper from all the different ministries included in the program. I was like thank you Lord," another member of the usher board told someone.

"Girl, check this out. I arrived at church today for usher duty, and Tyrone tells Angela and me that we're escorting everyone to their seat today and to smile. What a change. He also told us we're getting new uniforms, but wants to talk to the pastor about the church paying half. There will be three in total."

Tyrone saw Joanne and walked up to her.

"First Lady, how are you today?"

"I'm well. I've been hearing of all the changes you made today. Are they here to stay?"

"As long as the pastor is here, it will be that way for both services. The pastor's vision is in full force. I need to go now; have a good day."

Brenda was sitting in a chair across the room. She made eye contact with the first lady. They stared at each other, smiled, dipped their cup and then turned away. The first lady and Matthew started walking toward the pastor's office and just as they were approaching the door, it opened and the Chairman of the Board of Trustees, James McDonald, and the City Manager, George Logan, walked through. As soon as they saw Matthew Andrew Doorsill, whose nickname was MAD, their jaws dropped as if they were looking at a ghost, or a dear on the road staring at the headlights of a car. Brenda Cumming noticed the unanticipated look on the two men's faces, which made her curious. James and George were once members of Carroll's thuggish crew.

****

Everyone slowly completed their breakfast and made their way to their respective Sunday school classes. Joanne and Matthew attended the senior adult class for ages 30 and up. Trustee, James McDonald, was scheduled to teach Sunday school class. The day's lesson was about Community of Confession, taken from the Book of Nehemiah 9:1-37. James McDonald walked in the classroom and there were 12 students waiting for him to start class. The only person James noticed was Matthew Arden Doorsill. James approached the small, narrow podium in the center of the classroom, opened the class with a prayer, and then started teaching.

While he was teaching, the only thing he could think of was Matthew Doorsill taunting him. Matthew's presence alone inside the church was not good. James started asking himself a million questions, such as: why was he there, was he and the first lady talking about him, does she know about his past? However, he pushed forward and then brought the class to an end. As everyone exited Sunday school and headed toward the sanctuary for the noon service, James rushed to the restroom and vomited in the toilet. He was sick and his stomach was in knots. James knew he should go home, but he cleaned himself up and proceeded to the sanctuary for service.

As James was leaving the restroom, he bumped into his long-time high school friend and City Manager, George Logan.

"Boy, you're not looking good. What's wrong with you?"

"Do you remember me telling you I have a dark side that I can't shake, but I'm going to counseling for help?"

"Yeah, like five years ago. Why?"

"That man walking with the first lady is a judge who resided over a federal case that included me. Now I feel like she knows about my personal business. I was hoping that part of my life stayed in the past…deep in the past. The crime happened when I lived in the Miami, Florida area. That's why I moved here to Jacksonville, to put that lifestyle behind me."

"Wow, since we're confessing, I know him as well, and yes, he knows my dark secret and my parents. I see why we have such a kindred spirit. We have more in common than we assumed. I was living outside of Orlando, in the Kissimmee area and he was the judge on a case I was a part of as well."

Unbeknownst to each other, James McDonald and George Logan were arrested in a child pornography ring, which included more than 100 people from Savannah, Georgia to Miami, Florida. The ring was taking runaway teenagers and using them to create child pornography videos, which included boys having sex with one another, as well as with girls, and girls having sex with one another. The circle created and distributed the videos around the world. When arrested, James and George, with the help of Carroll Benson, a reformed gangster, provided evidence to the Department of Justice which resulted in discovering six additional child pornography rings around the United States and in the Caribbean. In return, the judge, Mathew Arden Doorsill, gave them a ten-year probation period.

"James, you look puzzled?"

"I am. My wife and children, the church and the community will discover what I did, what do we do?"

"The same thing that Beverly, Charlene, and Tyrone have done."

"What is that?"

"Support the pastor's vision and surrender. I'm certain after our last meeting, he was pushed to his limit. I was really slamming him. Everyone in the meeting badgered him."

"You think it will work?"

"If it doesn't, we're really in trouble. Red carpet service from this minute forward."

"I'm okay with that. Between you and I, I really like the pastor and his wife," James admitted.

The First Lady

"Church service is about to start."

James and George shook hands as if to say we have a deal, walked into the sanctuary, and each took a seat next to their wives. The choir was finishing their opening songs. The church's clerk had made the announcement for the week. The ushers had escorted everyone for the collection of tithes and offerings. The pastor completed altar call and the choir had song their last song. The pastor had been preaching now for about twenty minutes from the book of Job. The day's message was, "Are You Ready To Be Used By GOD?"

"…The Lord did not ask Job for permission. Job was not given a vote in the conversation between the Lord and Satan, nor was Job's children, servants, or wife. Job was not given a year, a month, a week, or even a day to prepare himself for what the Lord needed him for. Moreover, the Lord did not go into prayer mode before offering up Job in the conversation. But Yahweh knew, that he knew, that he knew, that he knew, that Job was ready to be used. He was committed to the Lord and would not disappoint him. The question for you today is, are you ready to be used by the Lord?" The pastor stopped preaching and looked around. Everyone in the church was quiet.

"I am walking down your street today and getting ready to knock on your door. It is easy to say I love Jehovah when your children are doing all the right things. It is easy to say I love El Olam when you have more than what you need. It is easy to say I love El Shaddai when you are in good health, and it is easy to say I love Elohim when everything in your life is perfect. But can you say it when it all has been taken away? If your wife leaves you, your children die in a car crash, you get fired from your job tomorrow, and the bank is foreclosing on your home, can you still say I love you Lord Jesus!"

From the pulpit, the pastor looked at his wife for a nod of approval as he always did when preaching. The first lady nodded her head to signal good job, you're looking good, sounding good, and I love you. The pastor was happy to receive her affirmation. To him, Joanne's approval was like someone saying to an attack dog, 'sic 'em.' The pastor had more words than time. He'd been preaching almost 30 minutes. He learned as a young preacher in Seattle that if you keep people too long, they may not come back next Sunday. But he was on fire and the spirit of the Lord was running hot within.

"Now Job, a devout man, feared God, did no evil, and stayed away from evil. He was a Godly man, a servant of the Lord Almighty, a good and caring father and husband. He did not sin; he prayed daily and made a sacrifice to the Lord for himself and each of his children. Even so, he suffered much from the lost of his loved ones – his children, his wealth, his livestock, as well as pain d– boils and more. Even after all that God permitted Satan to do to Job; Job did not once deny his love for the Lord. The devil caused all of Job's trouble, not God. God simply permitted it to happen. What you need to know now is just as Satan caused Job's tribulations, he will afflict you as well."

"Do not be fooled and think it cannot and will not happen to you. You are not exempt. Do not be fooled into thinking this is a story that happened thousands of years ago and has no merit to today's living. If we fast forward a few thousand years from Job to Luke 22:31, the Prince of Peace told Simon that the prince of confrontation had asked to sift him as wheat. Here is a message for someone. Satan is still asking for permission to destroy people. He is asking for you. Jesus told Peter, I have prayed that your faith does not fail you. Did you hear that, Jesus told Peter, Satan has asked for you and I have given you up, and I am praying that you believe in me and you will not fail."

"Jesus ended with this, 'When you return, strengthen your brothers.' When you are ready to be used by God, get ready because you will be used. God is praying that with the faith you have in Him, you will overcome the challenges of Satan.

Job, Peter, and many more have overcome the prince of darkness. With faith in God, you as well will be victorious."

Everyone in the church stood to their feet and gave the pastor a standing ovation. They were happy with the day's message. People in the church were talking to each other as the pastor wiped the perspiration from his face and took a drink of water.

"That's my time, but I need you to bear with me for a few more minutes because I have a few announcements. If you haven't heard, Jason Harrison and I will be competing in the Jacksonville Ironman Triathlon in a few weeks." Everyone stood again, clapping their hands. They knew it was something Jason had been working toward for years and his mother had asked a few men in the church to do the race with her son. "I will be out of town for about two weeks to get myself in shape for the race, so I've asked the First Lady to teach Bible study in my absence. She will teach on submission and revenge. I'm asking everyone to please come out and show your support. I assure you all, you will be blessed by her teaching. Now I would like Jason and his mother to come forward for a special prayer as we prepare for the big, upcoming race."

Evelyn and her son, Jason, rose from their seats and walked to the center of the church. Everyone was looking at how attractive Evelyn was. She had long, black, curly hair, and stood 5'9" with the perfect measurements – 36-24-36. She was wearing three inch, black and tan shoes, and a one-piece, long, black and beige sleeveless dress, which accentuated all of her curves. The eyes of every woman and man were on Evelyn; she was looking good and everyone knew it. The ladies slowly looked at the First Lady then turned to look at Evelyn. They were attempting to gauge Joanne's reaction, but her eyes were forward. She didn't look to the left nor the right. Unlike most ladies in the church, Joanne showed no sign of hate or intimidation of other attractive women. Just as Jason and his mother were almost to the pastor, Pastor McCoy called out to his wife.

"First Lady, will you please join us."

Joanne was sitting on a front row. She stood to her feet, took about three steps then stood next to the pastor. Evelyn reached Joanne and then both ladies hugged and gave each other a kiss on the cheek.

Chapter Five

The Plot

"Hello, how may I help you?" Angie Long asked, as she answered her cell phone.

"Angie, are you home?" Brenda replied.

"Yes, you okay?"

"I'm well. Is your husband home also?"

"Yes, are you sure you're okay?"

"Yes, stop asking me that. I'm almost at your house; I'll be there in a minute," Brenda said as she disconnected the call, exited off of I-295 and proceeded to W. 8th Street and then to Walnut Street, arriving at the home of Willie and Angie Long. Angie saw Brenda parking her car and walked outside.

Brenda, Angie, Willie, and Willie's younger brother, Malcolm, all attended William Raines Senior High School. Brenda and Malcolm dated while in school and Brenda and Angie had been the best of friends since elementary. Willie was about three years older than Brenda, Angie, and Malcolm. Willie met Angie more than 20 years prior; they married and had been happily married from day one. Brenda and Malcolm often took credit for the couple's relationship. Willie was a Deputy for the Jacksonville Sheriff's Department and his younger brother, Malcolm, was a police officer in the Atlanta, Georgia area.

"Brenda is there a problem with you?" Angie asked.

"I told you to stop asking me that. I'm fine. Where is your husband?"

"On the couch, watching the evening news."

"Thanks, I need to talk to him, now."

Brenda and Angie walked inside the house and into the living room. Willie was sitting in his oversized La-Z-Boy lounge chair, watching and enjoying his wall-mounted, sixty-one inch, flat screen, Samsung Smart TV.

"Willie, we need to talk."

"Good evening to you too," Willie replied.

"Good evening."

Angie sat on the sofa next to her husband's chair. Brenda sat in the middle of the sofa, facing Willie. Willie turned the volume down on the TV.

"Really Willie." Brenda turned and looked at him as if to say please turn it off. "Volume control; is that the best you can do?"

"Okay, let me go first. How can I help you?" Willie slowly asked Brenda. All the while he was thinking, "*You need to get out of my house!*"

It's church business. As Chairman of the Deacons and my Deacon, this is something for you."

"So this isn't personal…this is church business, right?"

"Yeah, I would not be bringing my personal problems to you or anyone else in the church for that matter. If I need help, I'll be going to see a professional, not an overnight Christ wannabe."

"Wannabe," Willie replied in a low voice so that Brenda couldn't hear him. "Whatever, what can I do for you?"

"Whomever we paid to do the investigation on the pastor and first lady robbed us. We should demand our money back and pay someone else."

Willie looked at his wife; his expression read, "*Do you hear this?*"

"That's not going to happen."

"Why?"

"Why are you here asking me that?"

"You're the Chairman of the Deacons and was Chairman of the Pastor Search Committee. So this is something you need to fix."

"Slow down; now pump your brakes and take a step back. Everyone present at the church meeting had one vote. And on that day, approximately 90% of the members were in attendance."

"So what? A mistake was made and you need to fix it."

"What is your problem today?"

"The first lady. There is more to her than you may think. The woman is a thug and a bitch! She's been blackmailing people in the church."

"What! Where do you come up with this information?" Willie looked at his wife as if to say, "*Why is your friend talking to me?*"

"Willie, I'm very serious. Please think about this. First Beverly, then Charlene, and now my husband, Tyrone. One by one, each person who spoke against the pastor has changed their viewpoint. They've transitioned from not supporting the pastor to selling out. The pastor gets whatever he wants."

"Babe, she's right about that," Angie interjected.

"But why do you think it's the first lady? Why don't you think it's the pastor? A new investigation is not going to happen. We spent enough time and money searching for a pastor. No additional funds will be spent by the church."

"It is her. She's a blackmailer, a thug, and a bully."

"Did you ask Tyrone why he made a change overnight? What she said to him?"

"She didn't say anything to him and his situation is different."

"She didn't say anything to him, but she blackmailed him…okay."

"Trust me, something isn't right and we were robbed. Please trust me. It's only a matter of time before you have a change of heart."

"Me, why is that?"

"The Board of Directors, the Deacons, and Trustees are blocking the pastor's vision. You sit on all three of those boards. She's going to get to one or all four of you guys - James, George, Jermaine, and or you. So I'm telling you now, if you have any dark secret and want it to stay dark and in the past, you cannot wait for the pastor to quit. You must find another way to get rid of him."

Willie looked at his wife. They also had a few family secrets they didn't want exposed. However, he was confident the pastor would quit soon.

"James, Chairman of the Trustees, George, the City Manager, and Robert, the Mayor, have a concrete plan to get rid of him. He'll be gone in a few weeks, and I'm certain as he spends time with Jason, there will be rumors about him and Evelyn soon."

James and Robert were once members of Carroll's gang of illegal activies. James was tall and very good looking, with a speech impediment. He'd been married and divorced three times at the age of forty-five and had two sons, both are currently in college at Howard University. Robert is a short man that talks fast. Although he has a history of illegal actives he also earned his Master degree in Political Science, his vision is to one day become a U.S. Senator and the Governor of Florida.

"James and George have fallen or will soon."

"Why do you say that?"

"Sunday in church, did you see the man the first lady was sitting with?"

"Yes, Matthew Doorsill. He's the Head Justice of the Supreme Court for the state of Florida. He was once a local councilman and then became the DA here in Jacksonville. I think he is a federal Judge in the Tallahassee, Florida area. Why?"

"Well I saw fear cross both their faces on Sunday. Trust me, they wet their pants when they saw him, so don't be surprised if they both reverse their opinions at an upcoming meeting."

Willie was looking around and thinking. Brenda was really getting his attention.

"The committee to search for a new pastor was given one year and $15,000. We searched for two years and spent more than $50,000 looking for the perfect, African American pastor. For the community it was sad, but we voted and selected a white pastor, you know how embarrassing that would be if that information gets out to the public."

"It was a mistake. An honest mistake," Brenda replied.

"No! It was us bargain basement shopping and being selective, two terms that should not be used in the same sentence. I told the people there was no perfect pastor, there are no perfect people, but I like the pastor. He's a good teacher and preacher," said Angie. Willie and Brenda looked at Angie as she expressed her feelings.

"Listen. When the church created the Pastor Search Committee, we were given one year and $15,000. When we started approaching two years and $50,000, a decision had to be made. We had to decide on a cut-off date and select from the 30 to 40 people who had visited the church."

"And we selected someone who didn't physically attend the church. At least from the ones who visited, we knew they were black," Brenda said.

"How did you vote?" Willie asked Brenda as he patiently awaited an answer he was not going to receive.

"This is funny. We only have ourselves to blame. We didn't want to cover his travel expenses. Therefore, we asked for a CD. We played the CD and liked what we heard. Our equipment was not working properly. Later, we discovered someone had removed a cable, so we weren't able to view the video. But we liked what we heard. He sounded black and we voted for him. In fact, 90% of the people voted for him. And within three days of his arrival, we started plotting how to get rid of him," Angie conveyed.

"Willie, please do this. Ask your brother to look into the pastor's past. Maybe he can find some dirt we can take to the board and force him to leave."

"Malcolm is in Georgia, not Washington State," replied Willie.

"I know that, but he's been a police officer for some years. He should know someone he can call, he should have some contacts," Brenda declared.

"Well you know a few years ago, he was at the FBI Academy for training," Angie added.

"I'll call him, but I'm not feeling this. Why don't you call him?" Willie asked Brenda.

"No, it's best if it comes from you."

"Brenda, the man has been happily married for some years. He's over you."

"You men are so naïve. You call him. It's best, trust me," Brenda stated as she stood up. "I need to run, but we must talk soon."

"I'll walk you out," Angie told Brenda. The women walked out of the room toward the front door to exit the home.

"Girl, next time you and your man are copulating, spray the house or open a window before you allow someone to come into your home," Brenda told Angie.

"First of all, we didn't invite you. Secondly, we were rendering due benevolence to one another."

"Bye girl, you still crazy," Brenda giggled as she got into her car and drove off.

****

"Good evening ladies. I don't know why we're meeting, but after I enjoy a crab slider, a side order of wings, a Sam Adams beer, and a Ginger Ale soda, I'm out of here and you two are paying the bill, so lets make this quick," Demetrius said to Sofia and Coleen. "Ma'am, I'm ready to order," Demetrius informed the waitress at the Eight Burger Bar & Sports Lounge located inside the Amelia Island's Ritz Carlton hotel. Astonished, Sofia and Coleen glared at Demetrius. The waitress came over and Demetrius placed his order. Sofia and Coleen ordered sweet potato fries and a soft drink each.

"We need your help." Sofia requested.

"I'm listening," Demetrius responded.

Demetrius, as well as his brother and sister was raised by their grandaunt. He knew his parents and spent a lot of quality time with the both of them. They stayed in trouble with the law enforcement community from the local, stated and federal levels. Demetrius father was once known as the biggest hoodlum in the state of Florida. He was never arrested or worked a nine-to-five, but he and his wife lived a very comfortable lifestyle in the Tallahassee Florida area. With the exception of Demetrius' choice for a lover, everyone that knows him and his father said they are exactly the same person, good looking, smart, and smooth talkers. It is also rumored that Carroll got his start as a criminal from Demetrius' father. Demetrius is the first person the First Lady befriended after she relocated to Jacksonville. While shopping in Publix, Demetrius approached Joanne and told her to come to his salon, so he could fix the tracks in her hair. She quickly explained to him with an attitude that she did not have tracks in her hair. After a few words of sarcasm towards each other they departed with hate towards each other. After inquiring from the local ladies about a good hair salon in the area, Joanne quickly ran into Demetrius a second time. And they quickly became friends.

"We need dirt, some help with Pastor McCoy…" Before Coleen could finish talking, Demetrius started laughing.

"What's funny?" Coleen asked.

"It's not going to happen. Joanne is my friend. Even if she wasn't, I have no dirt to share with you ladies."

"Come on D, I know you can give us something," Sofia pleaded.

"I can't help you ladies on this one."

"What about his schedule, what gym he goes to, when is he home alone? Give us something!" Sofia inquired more aggressively.

"I can't help and that's all I have to say on the matter."

"D, I feel like this could be a lucrative payoff. Please find out something for us!" Sofia was becoming more forceful with each request she made of Demetrius.

"I have no enemies within that family; leave me out of your cloak and dagger, get rich scams."

"What! You have no enemies, so this is what it's all about!? You used us to destroy your enemies. You fed us information so we could expose those you disliked!" Coleen snapped.

"What are you talking about girl?" Sofia inquired.

"Those pastors, local and state politicians, the CEOs, they are all anti-gay. Sofia, think about it; they all openly spoke out against gay rights. We were used to advocate for gay rights for D and his same-sex lover friends. What a fool we've been!"

The First Lady

Sofia, Coleen, and Demetrius all grew up in an area called Baldwin; they knew each other all their lives. For the past seven to eight years, Demetrius had been feeding information to Sofia and Coleen that helped them scam countless expensive gifts from various companies, churches, and individuals.

"D, look at me. Is this true?" Demetrius was eating his food.

Demetrius was used to people in the church, moreso Pastors and Fist Ladies, treating him differently since he was gay. However, he loved the fact that Joanne never looked at him or treated him differently; which resulted in their relationship developing into a true friendship.

"Ladies, we all won. I didn't use either of you; we all profited and acquired what we were after."

"No! Not all of us! You sat in the background and sent us out to the frontline to fight the battle for you and your gay friends!" Coleen retorted furiously.

"I taught you two how to play the game; I educated you on the skills of being a hustler – a very good one. You guys were on the battlefield, trying to hustle men of power for their money years before I joined your team."

"You used us!" Coleen was heated.

"How many times have you ladies been in a fist fight, before me? Before me, how many times were you chased, stabbed, sued, locked up, or your cars damaged and homes broken into? Now think about how many times it happened after I educated you on the art of being a hustler? The answer is none."

"It's not fair D! You used us! We're all supposed to be friends." Sofia countered.

"And we can keep on being friends, but to help you ladies with Pastor McCoy is a no. If you two are successful, more power to you, but keep me out of it."

"You gay bastard! You used us and wasn't man enough to admit it!" Coleen was livid.

"Tell me Coleen, how many blow-jobs did you give to get that Mercedes-Benz you drive daily? What is it, a SL-class, two-door roadster? None, I think is the correct answer. And you Sofia, how many did you give to get the Jaguar XKR convertible? I'm sure the answer is none. How many men did you ladies spread your legs for, for all of the expensive gifts you have, such as diamonds, mink furs, copper bathtubs, Vividus mattresses, two to three time shares each, and the trips to Africa, Europe, Japan, and China. The answer is none. Let's not forget the hundreds, maybe millions of dollars you two have in stocks and cash in various bank accounts. You look at me as if I don't know about your payoffs, expensive gifts, stocks, and bank accounts. I even know about your condos at Beau Rivage. You spend as much time as I do in the gym; and in the hair business, you learn things from people. You want a tip? Here's one for you, stay away from Joanne McCoy, she is not an easy prey. She's not your average pastor and or CEO's wife. She will fight back; and trust me, it will not be clean."

Sofia and Coleen merely looked at each other.

"I'm not running away," Coleen spoke up.

"Same here," Sofia agreed.

"Good luck ladies." Demetrius rose from his chair, walked out of the restaurant into the hotel lobby, and out of the hotel.

"So what do you think?" Sofia asked Coleen.

"Jerome McCoy is just another man with eyes and a penis, and his wife is another insecure woman. I'm going to take them both. You in or out?

"I'm in," Sofia affirmed.

****

"How do you feel knowing you're playing games with one of Jesus' followers?" Brother Calvin said to Brother David as the two families were walking from the parking lot toward the church for Bible study.

"Baby girl, you can walk ahead," David said to his daughter as he talked to Calvin. "Brother, why are you giving me a hard time? I believe in the word and I believe in Jesus Christ. I also believe that some things in the Bible are not properly understood and are only intended for a specific time and purpose in history. I just hate when these preachers try to connect everything in the Bible to current day. I don't think it's possible. Some things need to stay five and ten thousand years in the past, that's all I am saying."

"I still think you were wrong for setting up the pastor like that."

"Well if I'm wrong, he'll win or finish the race. If I'm right, he'll lose and not finish."

"Are you for real? About 40 to 60 percent of the people don't finish."

"What percent of that is walking around saying, I can do all things in Christ, huh?"

"Open the door, please."

"Right, I hope his wife is smarter."

Calvin and David entered the church for Wednesday night Bible study.

"You see that?" Brenda asked Willie about James and George. As the two families approached the church for Bible study, James and George were in the far corner of the parking lot having a private conversation.

"Two men talking, wow?" Tyrone replied.

"Yes, step aside!" Brenda told her husband, Tyrone as she walked closer to Willie.

"What do you think?" Willie asked Brenda.

Willie's wife and Tyrone entered the church, while Angie and Willie were on the steps talking.

"They're plotting. Their time is limited and soon they'll be like Charlene and Beverly."

"And Tyrone," Willie added.

"Right, did you talk to Malcolm?"

"Yes, he said he has a police friend in Washington State. But if she is what you think, this thing has the potential of backfiring and can be dangerous."

"Just tell him to move quickly. I need to get in for Bible study. Hate to miss this," Brenda said as she turned and walked into the church. James and George were walking toward one of the side doors of the church.

"You know, I'm not feeling this plotting thing," James told George.

"I agree with you, but I feel like we have no choice. She drew first blood. We're men protecting our families and our church family," George responded.

"I'm like you, what happened in the past needs to stay in the past. What happened 10 years ago, doesn't define the people we are today. We're men of the Lord Almighty, serving our church and community."

"Do you think this will work?" James asked.

"Dude, check this out. My neighbor works at the same hospital Evelyn works at. He tells me she's always telling the ladies in the hospital how horny she is and how long it's been since she's been with a man. One day, the pastor will pickup or drop off Jason, and I'm sure she will either jump his bones or he'll go for her. Trust me, if Potiphar's wife looked as good as Evelyn, the story of Joseph running from her would be different in the Bible. No matter what, my man will start a rumor about the two of them. Trust me he's good; it will damage the two of them," George stated emphatically.

George's neighbor didn't attend Abundant Truth Baptist Church, didn't know Evelyn, nor did he work at the same place as Evelyn. The communication between the two men was disjointed.

"Sounds like a small chance of being successful, but we'll see. With all honesty, I think we should act as if it's nothing. After all, he can't talk about what he knows is illegal. It's the law" said James.

"Well if the rumors don't work, I have a friend who's a retired FBI agent. I'll call him to get some trash on the couple. Trust me, they played their hand. It's my turn now."

After their conversation, the two men walked into the church.

Chapter Six

Revenge Lesson

Comfortable seating capacity for Abundant Truth Baptist Church was approximately 300 people. On most Sundays, the church averaged roughly 75 people during morning service and an estimated 100 individuals at the noon service. Wednesday night Bible study averaged about 25 students. Since Pastor McCoy took leadership of the church approximately four months prior, attendance had increased by 25% for both services as well as Bible study.

On this night, there were more than 100 people at Bible study. Word had spread throughout the community that the pastor with a PhD in Theology had left the congregation in the hands of the first lady with a hair school certificate. Rumor had also got out that she was a biker, which made people exceedingly curious as to what they had been hearing about her. Many people came to see her fail. On the other hand, there were many who knew the hearts of some folk. Thus, they attended to provide moral support.

It was 7:00 p.m. The First Lady walked to the podium, wearing dark blue jeans and a white, short sleeve sweater with low, two-inch heals. At 5'9'', she had a sexy figure in jeans and heels. Joanne looked out into the sanctuary, observing the increase in attendance. She also detected Kalevi sitting in the sanctuary with three of his friends. Normally, Kalevi sat alone in the rear of the church in the middle of the pew. Both people from the church, as well as the community, avoided Kalevi due to his disheveled appearance and offensive odor. Fortunately, he was among friends, not church members. Joanne also noticed Sofia and Coleen in the church; and she was surprised to see them since the pastor wasn't present. Joanne opened Bible study with a simple prayer.

"Let us pray, 'My Lord and My God, who can do anything but fail and or lie, the one and only Almighty God, I submit myself to you as a servant. Use me now; talk to me and through me so your people can receive a positive word from you tonight. This is not about me; it is all about you. Amen.'"

Everyone in the church said amen. Joanne was standing between two easels located in the front of the church.

"When we think about seeking revenge, what does the Bible tell us about revenge?" Joanne asked the warm bodies seated comfortably on the church pews. Everyone was surprised. They were not accustomed to the teachers of Bible study asking questions, especially at the beginning of service. Therefore, everyone was quiet.

"This is not a trick question. If you have your Bibles, please use them," Joanne requested.

"Vengeance is mine!" Brenda yelled.

"Thank you," said Joanne as she walked to the easel and wrote the scripture on the white paper. "Romans 12:19 says, 'Dearly beloved, avenge not yourselves, but rather give place unto wrath: for it is written, Vengeance is mine; I will repay, saith the Lord'." The warm bodies sitting upon the benches were in shock that Joanne quoted the scripture correctly. "More please."

"Matthew 5:43-48 says, 'You shall love your neighbor and hate your enemy.' But I say to you, Love your enemies and pray for those who persecute you, so that you may be sons of your Father who is in heaven. For He makes His sun rise on the evil and on the good, and sends rain on the just and on the unjust. For if you love those who love you, what reward do you have? Do not even the tax collectors do the same? And if you greet only your brothers, what more are you doing than others? Do not even the Gentiles do the same'?" A member of the church read from their Bible.

"Thank you," replied Joanne as she wrote the scripture on the white paper.

"Ephesians 4:31-32!" Willie, the Chairman of the Deacons yelled.

"Let all bitterness and wrath and anger and clamor and slander be put away from you, along with all malice. Be kind to one another, tenderhearted, forgiving one another, as God in Christ forgave you." Joanne quoted as she wrote the scripture on the white paper. Again, the people were flabbergasted by her knowledge. "More please," she called out firmly as though she was a professor in a college setting.

Everyone in the church was quiet. Many who had only come to watch her fail were surprised at her ability to quote scriptures. Joanne walked to the board and began writing and talking. She directed the bible study members, "Please write down these scriptures and read them for homework:

Luke 6:31–And as you wish that others would do to you, do so to them.

Romans 12:1–I appeal to you therefore, brothers, by the mercies of God, to present your bodies as a living sacrifice, holy and acceptable to God, which is your spiritual worship.

Mark 11:25–And whenever you stand praying, forgive, if you have anything against anyone, so that your Father also who is in heaven may forgive you your trespasses.

Matthew 15:18-19–But what comes out of the mouth proceeds from the heart, and this defiles a person. For out of the heart come evil thoughts, murder, adultery, sexual immorality, theft, false witness, slander.

Ephesians 4:32–Be kind to one another, tenderhearted, forgiving one another, as God in Christ forgave you.

Okay, I think that is enough for us to get started, unless someone has more they would like to add."

Joanne paused to give everyone a chance to respond. With her captivating personality and comprehension of the Bible, Joanne reduced her haters by 75% within the first 15 minutes of Bible study.

"Okay, we'll move on by reading Matthew 5:39, 'But I say unto you, that ye resist not evil: but whosoever shall smite thee on thy right cheek, turn to him the other also.' I know this is a scripture that is familiar to everyone, so I ask you, what do you think this scripture is teaching?"

"How to be humble," replied one of the church members.

"Thank you, I have a story for you all. As far as I can remember, at about the age of five years old, my parents, mostly my father made us – my brother, sister, and I read the Bible daily. Each year from the age of five to about 16 or 17 years old, we all read the entire Bible, reading anywhere from two to four chapters a day. So in my home, we knew the Bible, but we didn't necessarily comprehend the words. In Seattle, my family is large, very large. I have a brother and sister and my father has five brothers and three sisters. I think my grandfather has four sisters and six brothers and my great-grandfather has nine brothers. Yes, my great-grandfather only had boys, no girls. At the McKinney family reunions, which is my maiden name, there are easily more than five hundred in attendance and most of them are still in the Seattle area."

"If you go to Seattle and ask anyone about the McKinney family, you will get to my people. The sad thing about growing up there is no matter what we did, some family member was around and word always got back to my father. I tell you this, go any place in Seattle; throw a rock in any direction, and you'll hit someone in my family. So one day at church, my younger brother, Darrell, got in a fight in the church. He beat-up the pastor's son, Leroy Brown."

"I will never forget that day. It really opened my eyes to understanding the words of the Bible. My father and the pastor, Leroy Brown, Sr., tried talking to the boys by asking them what Jesus said about someone hitting you. My brother

76

said, 'I did as the Bible said. Am I getting a beating?' Being humble were the words they were looking for. However, that wasn't Darrell's response. Now place a pin there; we'll come back to this story."

Brenda and Willie looked at each other; everyone looked like they were really enjoying the lesson.

"Now we live in a society of exceptional power: the one with the strongest fists or the most guns wins. Instead of the Golden Rule, our ethics are, 'Do unto others first, before they do unto you. If they do anything bad to you at all, finish them off before they can do anything worse.' Or my personal favorite, 'I don't get mad, I get even.' All of these expressions are of human, normal response. However, to be a follower of Christ, you and I are called to live a different lifestyle – to love without limits. When we accomplish this goal, we are like God himself."

"Disagreeing to popular saying, we have no rights in God's Kingdom."

"Albeit there is a law for retaliation in the Old Testament, 'An eye for an eye, and a tooth for a tooth.' In the book of Exodus and Deuteronomy, you can read how pay back was permissible. Nevertheless, it was limited by setting restrictions. The law was intended as an equalizer of justice. If a person knocks out my tooth, I get his. And if I poke out his eye, he gets mine. Retaliation as we know it sets out to go beyond that. We want to up the ante. We want two eyes for an eye or a life for an eye. But Old Testament law limited disproportionate revenge."

"In other words, people could only get back what they lost. In addition to being merciful, the law limited revenge for the offended. It didn't allow the whole family to get into the act. When wronged, we tend to line up forces of family and friends to strike back. If a person cuts off my ear, I want to cut off his head. And if I cut off his head, his brother will kill me, and if he kills me, my brother will kill his brother, and pretty soon we have a clan war. Without the law of retaliation, revenge extends from the individual to the family, to the clan to the tribe, and ultimately, to entire nations. Subsequently, what seems like a blood-hungry law was actually a way of limiting violence and bloodshed. Furthermore, while the law allows one to get even within limits, it does not require one to get even as they desire."

"Jesus's teaching goes above and beyond the law. Jesus said do not retaliate against an evil person. Here, Jesus is talking about revenge, not self-defense. He isn't telling us to be weak and passive; He's telling us not to be vindictive. Jesus wants us to ask the question, 'If someone does something evil to me, how may I respond with only good in return'? Obviously, this is a high standard to live up to! Yet, Jesus' style of discipleship is not for spiritual wimps!"

"Jesus said, 'Whoever slaps you on your right cheek, turn the other to him also.' This verse is often used to prohibit any form of self-defense. But is this Jesus' intent? No. First of all, notice that Jesus specifically mentions 'the right cheek.' Approximately 90% of the people in the world are right-handed. I'm right-handed and if I punch you with my right hand, I will hit you on the left cheek. If I try to hit you on the right cheek with my right fist, I won't hurt you one bit. Jesus is not referring to a situation where another person is attempting to punch your lights out. He is speaking of a slap across the right cheek with the back of the right hand."

"Second, at that time, a slap to one's face was considered a gross insult by the Jews, and was among the most demeaning acts one could inflict on another person. Slapping someone on the cheek was a sign of contempt and did not pose a serious safety threat. It was considered a terrible insult. Receiving the back of the hand meant you were scorned as being inconsequential – a nothing. If a man struck you with the back of his hand instead of punching you in the mouth, you could collect twice the damages because an insult was worse than an injury. It was a society of honor-shame. Even today, the Irish often say, 'The back of my hand to you,' meaning you are scum."

"Third, Jesus is not describing a physical attack and telling us to roll over and play dead. We should not encourage our children to be beat up by bullies. Nor should we stand by and watch while an innocent person is attacked. We should not permit thieves, murderers, and terrorists to have their way in our society. When necessary, we should seek to protect ourselves, our family members, and victims of injustice and cruelty. But what Jesus is saying is this: When someone insults you, do not seek revenge. We should not trade insults, even if it means we receive more. We must avoid retaliation and personal revenge! When we love without limits, we're like God. Does anyone have a question?"

Each person was impressed with Joanne's teaching style.

"What happened to your brother?" a church member asked.

"Well, because my father made us read the bible daily, Darrell attempted to use it for his defense. My father had no clue what he was talking about. Hence, my father took him to the back room and put that leather belt on him. But I learned from my baby brother to turn the right cheek, and not just any cheek. Now when I read, I read slowly and think about the words."

Joanne concluded Bible study with a prayer. Evelyn and many others approached her and began a conversation, while others shared how they enjoyed the lesson and were surprised at the First Lady's level of knowledge and teaching skills. In the parking lot, Tyrone, Angie, Brenda, and Willie stopped by their cars and began a small conversation.

"Hey, if the first lady's people in Washington State are as large as she said, looking into her background could really backfire," said Willie.

"It's just talk, trust me. She's a bully and a hoodlum. She talks trash to make herself sound as if she's all that. She's a simple, urban living country girl from the hood of Seattle trying to make herself sound big in Florida as if all blacks in the south are dumb and slow," Brenda expressed.

"Brenda and I talked about this and I think we should back off. Willie, you should tell your brother to drop the background investigation. I don't have good vibe about this," Tyrone added.

"I agree with Ty. She may be a bully and a thug, but I don't think it's worth the risk. Besides, I like the pastor and his wife. In all honesty, things have been looking good for the short time they've been here. So what if he's white! We learn in the Bible to look into the inner person, not the outer person," Angie announced.

The four were looking at each other, but no one was talking.

"Well since you already asked, let's see what happens," Brenda suggested. Tyrone was surprised by what his wife said. Just a day before, they agreed to ask Willie to ask his brother, Malcolm, to drop the inquiry into the first lady's background.

Lori Rickover saw Joanne and Kalevi talking in the parking lot and walked over to join them.

"I'm glad to see you and your friends in Bible study," Joanne informed Kalevi as they walked to her car.

"They said they enjoyed tonight and will come again to hear the pastor preach," Kalevi replied.

"May I help you?" Joanne asked Lori as Kalevi stood next to them. Lori looked at Joanne as if Kalevi was not in their presence.

"I'm in need of some handiwork around my home, mostly outside, do you know of anyone?" Lori asked.

"Travis…" Before Joanne could complete her statement, Kalevi cleared his throat.

Unbeknownst to Joanne, Kalevi and Lori had some history; they dated once in high school. After high school, Kalevi joined the Marine Corps in 1997 and served in both the Iraq and Afghanistan war between 2003 and 2010. After he returned home from the Corps with a medical discharge in 2010, Kalevi lived a homeless lifestyle, but never had a run-in with the law or the people in the community. Moreover, he never took his eyes off of Lori.

"Kalevi may be able to help; when do you need someone?" Joanne answered quickly.

"Saturday morning for about two to four hours. I need to get my yard ready."

Turning to Kalevi, Joanne asked, "You free?" In doing so she noticed how he was gazing at Lori. Kalevi nodded his head up and down in the affirmative.

"He will need your address," Joanne softly requested of Lori, who sauntered off to her car and drove away.

****

"Babe, social media is saying a lot of good stuff about Wednesday Night Bible Study at Abundant Truth Baptist Church. Great job!" Jerome congratulated Joanne. Jerome was at the Hilton Garden Inn located in Virginia Beach, Virginia across from Pembroke Mall.

"Thank you baby! How are things going up there in Virginia?"

"All is well. My body is truly hurting; but you know no pain, no gain."

"Someone who doesn't workout said that. I talked to Evelyn after Bible study. She is really excited about what you're doing for her son. It would be sad if she knew it was a result of deception, rather than a genuine deed."

"Right. That brother David, I wonder what his issue is," said Jerome.

"He's a single parent raising a young girl."

"And?"

"Just fishing for a reason. Hopefully, hanging around with Calvin, he will learn something."

"How are you settling in the First Lady position? Do you feel like the people are taking to you?" Jerome asked.

"Some are accepting me and some are not. They don't see a First Lady riding a motorcycle and wearing leather, but I'm okay with things. I see people changing daily; the new members seem to be receptive of my lifestyle."

"Cool, do you know why people at the church think you only have a hair school degree?"

"What the heck is a hair school degree?" Joanne asked then they both burst into laughter.

"These people think they are so smart and intelligent. They fail to realize how dumb they are. I've never heard of a hair school degree, it's cosmetology, beauty, and or hair styling school. I was wondering why everyone was looking at me as if I had two heads. I guess they didn't expect a person with a hair school degree to be intelligent enough to quote scriptures," Joanne retorted.

"No one on social media is talking about your BA degree in Psychology or your MA in Hospitality Business Management from the University of Washington. Now that's strange."

"But it explains why people have been acting so funny at times."

"Wow!"

"Babe, you remember Joanne McInnis, don't you? We all went to the same high school and she was arrested for robbing a local store when we were in our senior year?"

"The same girl people used to say looked like you and assumed you two were sisters?"

"Yes, the same one. She works in my Parkland hair salon and ..."

"You gave her a job!" Jerome yelled.

"Yes."

"When? I never knew this."

"Jerome, I told you. This goes to show how much you listen to me. Well she needed a new start. She's been working there since the store opened; she's been managing it now for about three years."

"You have an ex-con managing your business?"

"No, she never served time, and will you listen to me and stop interrupting, please?"

"Okay, I'm listening."

"I'm willing to bet the church hired a cheap investigator and he investigated her and not me. It all makes sense now. They used my maiden name and the wrong name."

"Well it would make sense as to why the church members are not fond of us. Anyway, before I forget, I need you to get some fresh flowers for Sunday and my flight lands around 8:00 p.m."

"Okay babe, you get your rest. I love you."

"I love you as well, babe. Also, go to Lowes or Home Depot and get a recycle bin for the church please. Time to go; 6:00 a.m. comes soon. Good night first lady."

"Good night pastor."

"Babe, did you receive the images I sent you?"

"Yes, someone sent you a picture of their breast and vulva?"

"What? Vulva?"

"Vagina, Jerome."

"So what do we do next?"

"We still don't know who sent the pictures, it's not like we can ID a person from those pictures, so we wait and act as if we never received them."

"Good night babe."

"Good night."

It was Friday night. Jerome and Joanne hung up the phone and went to sleep.

Chapter Seven

The Final Plot

It was Saturday afternoon. Joanne parked her car in the parking lot of Melody's Florist located on the corner of Main Street N. and W. 16th Street. She got out of her car, walked in the florist, and quickly noticed Coleen.

"Good afternoon Melody and Coleen," Joanne greeted them.

"First Lady, good afternoon. What a surprise to see you here," replied Coleen.

Melody didn't respond to Joanne, so Joanne said it a little louder. "Melody, hi, how are you today?"

"I'm well. Are you here for flowers for the church?"

"Yes, I would like something different from what the pastor's been getting once a week, something with a little purple and orange."

"I think he would like the red and yellow roses!" Coleen spat out; Joanne acted as if she didn't hear Coleen's suggestion.

"I received a large order of rainbow roses, how's that?"

"Let me get two dozen of those for the pastor's office and some large lilies and blue roses for the sanctuary."

"Not a problem. Are you waiting for them?"

"No, can I come back in about three hours?"

"First Lady, I can wait for them and deliver them to the church if you like?" Coleen shockingly volunteered.

"No thank you." Joanne replied smartly while wearing a smile.

"Sure, they'll be ready or I'll deliver them to the church myself."

"Thank you Melody. The pastor is out of town and he's running me crazy."

"Joanne," Melody said as she walked closer to Joanne. She didn't want anyone in the shop to hear their conversation. Melody continued by saying, "Hey, I've been very nice to you and the pastor. Do you think you can hook me up with his brother or cousin? Girl, I'm having a hard time meeting a good man and I've been praying hard."

"Melody, he's an only child."

"No way!"

"Yes, he is. I'll see you in a few hours."

"Thank you."

"Ms. Joanne, I heard that you're very busy; I would like to offer my assistance to you and the pastor."

"Like what; what type of assistance?"

"Maybe one day a week, I can run some errands, do some work around your home."

"Sister Coleen, thank you, but the pastor and I are fine. If you would like to assist, the community can use some volunteers. But word to the wise, never allow another woman into your home – ever." Joanne suggested as she smiled at Coleen and turned around to walk away.

"Why?" Coleen asked.

Joanne stopped and turned around, displaying her million-dollar smile, and in a nonchalant manner, she asked the question, "Do you know the story of the frog and the scorpion?"

"No, why do you ask?"

"You really need to study the story of the frog and the scorpion." Having said that, Joanne turned around, exited the shop, and got into her car.

Joanne departed the florist shop and headed over to Home Depot.

****

"Willie, this is Carroll. I'm calling a special meeting of the men. Can you meet today?"

Carroll was Brenda's older brother. They had the same father but different mothers. They grew up in different households. Both of them were born and raised in Jacksonville, Florida. Carroll was a high school dropout, and at one time was the largest gangster in the Jacksonville area. Between his 16th and 35th birthday, he had been incarcerated in penal institutions on multiply occasions for varying criminal activity; ranging from drugs, theft, prostitution, gambling, making and distributing sex videos, etc. Throughout Carroll's life, he served a total of twelve years in Florida prisons. He was now a well-respected businessman who owned six McDonalds; four Burger Kings; three Chick-fil-As; eight Popeye's; two KFCs; various Touchless Car Wash stations; two nightclubs; five car dealerships, where he is busy selling new and used cars. They were all in Jacksonville, Florida.

Carroll was in love with Evelyn Harrison. They dated for about three months, but after she learned about his criminal past, she decided she didn't want to continue to be associated with him. However, Carroll was determined to have a relationship with Evelyn; so he refused to accept no for an answer. The meeting that day was to implement his course of action to get rid of Pastor McCoy. Carroll viewed Pastor McCoy as a threat to him having a relationship with Evelyn.

From the rumors Carroll had been hearing, Joanne was a street smart, inner city girl from Seattle with a hair school certificate. She was a chick from the hood that rode a motorcycle, and was an aggressive thug and bully who lacked class. Conversely, Jerome was a handsome, white male with a doctoral degree and lots of class. Carroll believed Jerome would be a perfect match for Evelyn.

Although Carroll told people his former life as a gangster was behind him, there were rumors that he had many of the city's political officials from Brunswick, Georgia, to Kissimmee, Florida, under his influence.

"Sure, I can meet today. I'm heading to Home Depot now, but after that, what time and where?"

"In about two hours, my place, please."

"Okay, later brother."

"Later."

Willie was heading to Home Depot to purchase some parts to repair his lawn mower. As he located the parts he needed, he ran into Joanne who was there to purchase a recycle bin for the church.

"Joanne, how are you today? It's surprising to run into you here."

"I'm fine. The pastor sent me to purchase this recycle bin because he's tired of seeing cans and bottles in the trash."

"He should have told me; I would have gotten one."

"He said the Board of Directors would get one, but didn't want to wait. He's a green man; a recycler."

"Okay, well I need to run. I have a meeting to attend in about an hour."

"I understand, but I have a question for you," Joanne stated as she sat down the recycle bin and reached into her purse."

"Sure, what's on your mind?"

"Do you have a brother named Malcolm Jamal Long who is a police officer in the Atlanta Georgia area? I think he's a sergeant?"

Willie was flabbergasted; everything Brenda had said to him just came true.

"Yes."

"Please give him my number," Joanne requested as she handed him a business card. "I was told that he inquired about me. Please tell him he can call me directly." Willie accepted the card and then Joanne walked away. Willie paid for his parts, left the store, and called his brother.

"Malcolm, you okay?" Willie asked.

"Yes, why do you ask?"

"Did you get in any trouble from asking about that woman, Joanne McCoy?"

"No, I should have something in a few days."

"Brother, your point of contact sold you out. As of now, you've never heard of Joanne McCoy. You need to protect yourself and your career."

"What do you mean?"

"Joanne, she just handed me her phone number for you to call her. She said she heard you were inquiring about her and you can call her directly. Your contact in Seattle or someone just dropped your name and information to Joanne. Stay away from both of them."

"Really?"

"Yes, and if Brenda calls you, hang up on her. Listening to her got us in this mess."

"Okay, I got it. But who is this woman. I thought you said she was your first lady?"

"That's true, but there's more to her. I need to go now, but we will talk soon, later."

"Okay, bye."

"Bye."

"Ms. McCoy, how are you today?"

Joanne turned around to see who was calling her name, recognizing Sofia. At this point, she realized that Coleen and Sofia were personally feeling her out, which was upsetting her.

"Sofia, how are you?" Joanne slightly chuckled with a smile.

"What's funny?"

"I saw your friend, Coleen a few minutes ago. It's funny to see you both in such a short time frame."

Sofia realized that Joanne was aware of her and Coleen's game.

"Have a good day, Ms. McCoy. I need to run now." Sofia quickly departed Home Depot and returned home to start developing a plan to outsmart Coleen.

****

Willie, Chairman of the Deacons, parked his car outside of Carroll's home and walked in. He was surprised to see Robert Brunel, the Mayor; George Logan, the City Manager; James McDonald, Chairman of the Trustees; Tyron Cumming, President of the Usher Ministry and a member of the Trustees; Jermaine William, Chairman of the Board of Director and Danny Salesman, a Lieutenant at the police department, as well as other members of the church. The entire group consisted of men.

"Gentlemen, I'm happy you all were able to attend on such short notice. I've spoken with my baby sister, Brenda Cumming, and she has convinced me there are some issues at Abundant Truth Baptist Church. She has asked me to help and I've agreed."

Carroll didn't care who the Pastor at Abundant Truth Baptist Church was. He was only concerned for his own personal motive, which in this case, was protecting a relationship that didn't exist between him and Evelyn. Despite that, he wasn't planning on sharing that information with anyone.

"People, I know you all want to get rid of your pastor. I realize it would be better for him to depart by choice and quietly rather than the church ask him to leave. I also realize his departure must happen soon. From a business perspective, options are limited. Voting him out is not an option. Each week, people in the church are starting to accept him and his wife. Furthermore, since he's been at the church, membership has increased by 50%. So voting him out of office is not going to happen."

"At the Ironman race, he's going to come out looking like a hero. Even more people will like him; even if he only runs one mile. As soon as you connect a handicap person and a pastor in something like the Jacksonville Ironman Triathlon, he doesn't have to win or complete the race. People will love him for trying and he'll win their hearts. Finally, this plot about starting rumors that the pastor and Evelyn are having a relationship is stupid. There are two reasons why that won't work. Foremost, he and his wife are too smart for them to be alone with anyone, at anytime. Secondly, Evelyn is too popular at work, and George's neighbor, the person that's Evelyn's co-worker, is damaged goods. No one will listen to him."

"And if any of you think Sofia and Coleen is going to shake things up, my source told me their teacher, Demetrius, the gay man, who owns four or five hair salons in the area and is a weight lifter and body builder; is not behind them as he has been in the past, which means they will fail as well. No matter how many pictures those ladies send the pastor of their tits and twat, or how many rumors they start about what boys and girls he's sleeping with is useless. Unless you can attach a name and a face to those rumors and they can name a date, place, and time of opportunity, like that black pastor in Atlanta or that coach at Penn State College, it's a waste of time. But I have a new plan, one that will work in a few weeks."

"Carroll," said Robert Brunel as he stood from his chair. "We've all known each other for many years. Danny and I have given you all of our support because we're friends. But Danny and I are here to let you know we will no longer be involved with this plot. This four to six week conspiracy has gone on for too long. The man is not quitting; he has proven that he is not easily intimidated. In addition, the church is growing, so keep him. Let him be the pastor. Things can't get any worse from what I see."

"Danny, what about the police issuing tickets on Sunday?" Tyrone asked.

"If the cars are illegally parked, they will be ticketed. Good luck men and have a good day."

Robert and Danny walked out of Carroll's home, and then got into their respective vehicles and departed for their homes.

"Well back to business, men. Let me introduce you all to Dwight Landry. He is a retired FBI agent and I invited him to this meeting. Dwight and I have years of history. I came to trust him. He was a good investigation agent with the FBI. Although he's retired, he's still a good investigator. I think it's worth listening to what he has to say."

With a Heineken bottle in his right hand, Dwight stood up at 6'2" and weighed roughly 225 pounds. His dirty, blond hair was pulled back into a ponytail. He was sporting a shadow beard and goatee, and wearing blue jeans, and a long, pullover shirt.

"Men, Carroll explained all of your concerns and the mistake that was made. If you don't mind telling me yourselves what happened, I can assess how I can better assist," Dwight stated.

Everyone in the room was silent and looking at each other. No one wanted to speak up.

"Hey, I can explain things, but I've had a change of heart as well. The pastor and first lady should stay. I'm okay with them. I think we should reconsider this plot," Willie spoke up.

"Repent." Carroll whispered with a smile on his face.

"Brother, they need to go," said Tyrone as he looked at Willie. "They really need to go at any cost."

"Brother, I know you and many others have some dark secrets that you all want to keep in the past, and I get that. I have my own skeletons in the closet as well. But we have no proof that either of them have anything on any one of us," Willie declared.

"Waiting until it's public knowledge is not the right time to take action; the time for action is now! Willie, you were chairman on the Pastor Search Committee. Just tell him, you know more than any of us and you have copies of the investigator report," urged James.

"Okay," Willie said as he stood and took a deep breath. "I was the chairman, but keep in mind that everyone casted one vote. It's simple; The Board of Directors set the standards for the committee as far as locating a pastor. The qualifications included: married, Master's Degree, Degree in Theology, no online degree, between the ages of 30 and 35, plus or minus one year, and black. We were given a budget of $15,000 and one year."

"When we were pushing toward the end of year two and $50,000, the church members wanted us to make a decision. We were forced to end the search for the perfect pastor and select from those we had already interviewed. Each candidate came to the church for their trail sermon and a face-to-face meeting with church members. We didn't want to pay for Pastor McCoy and his wife to fly round-trip from Washington State to Jacksonville, Florida, because we were already close to $35,000 over-budget and one year beyond the established time frame."

"For that reason, we requested a CD/DVD. He sent us two. We all listened and enjoyed his preaching and teaching. Again, we listened. The video system was not operating properly so we were unable to view the video, only listen to the audio. Then we paid an investigator to examine his family. The only thing we didn't like was his wife's education, but we hired him anyway. We weren't overly concerned about the first lady's level of education because her position is not a very active role."

"The first lady is very active and productive at Abundant Truth Baptist Church and the community!," George yelled out, causing everyone to smile in agreement.

"Well once he arrived, we noticed his skin color, white with a black wife and most of the people were upset. We are an inner city church serving blacks in the community. Therefore, we believed a black pastor would be good to take the church to the next level, which we never defined. Now you have it. If we vote him out, we have to pay one year's salary, all medical and dental expenses as well as all moving expenses associated with him returning home. However, if he quits, we pay nothing."

"How much is that?" Carroll asked.

"Whatever we take in on fourth Sunday is his salary. Last month that was $13,500. Five months ago when he first arrived, it was short of $5,000," James acknowledged.

"So this is the status men. An in-depth background check costs money. If you choose to pay it, it's not going to be cheap. If you want information that is not on Google, or at the local courthouse, or at the DMV, it will cost to obtain it. And trust me, there is some information on this couple you want to get – trust me." Dwight repeated.

"Why do you say that?" Willie asked.

"I *Googled* the first lady and checked the DMV records and I can get family information on her. I did the same for your pastor, but no family information came up. Anyone who's breathing has a digital print. Pastor Jerome McCoy's digital print will cost you. Based on my work with the FBI, that information is normally good. Consequently, it has to be accessed beyond FBI databases, as well as the military, CIA, ATF, and DEA," Dwight informed them.

"You cannot be serious," George stated.

"I am; trust me, I am very serious," Dwight answered.

"Men, I'm putting up the first $10,000. I think we should do this." Carroll was onboard.

"That's a lot of money, but I'm in," James and George said in unison.

"How long will it take?" Willie queried.

"About four to six weeks, maybe less, maybe more, depending on what my contacts will do for me and how much they charge for their services."

Even though they were reluctant about the unknown fee, each individual agreed to pay the investigator. Afterwards, everyone slowly rose and went home.

****

Southwest flight 1221 landed at Jacksonville International. Joanne was waiting to welcome her husband and give him a ride home for the weekend. His plane would depart Jacksonville on Sunday evening. Disembarking the plane, before Jerome's eyes was his beautiful wife wearing open toe, black shoes with three-inch heels; along with a fitted, black dress, complimenting her 36-26-38 body measurements. The front was V-shaped; displaying her size 36 cleavage and her back was out. The dress came to the top of her knees. Joanne looked sexy; everyone in the waiting area was watching her. Spotting her husband, Joanne slowly and seductively sauntered in his direction as he advanced toward her. She leaned into his tall, handsome body and gave him a big, juicy kiss as her hands rested on his shoulder while his hands slowly and softly caressed her hips.

Timothy, the man who sat next to Jerome on the plane from Virginia to Florida, an older white male, pastors a church in the Kings Bay Georgia area. Timothy approached Jerome and his wife and then stopped and looked on as they kissed each other as if Jerome was a service man returning from a warzone overseas. Jerome stopped kissing his wife and made the introductions.

"Babe, this is Pastor Timothy Jackson. Timothy, this is my wife, Joanne." Timothy and Joanne shook hands and greeted each other. Because he was still bewildered by what he was seeing, Timothy had not said a word yet. It wasn't that Jerome was white and Joanne black. He had never seen a first lady dress so sexy and a pastor and a first lady display so much affection for one another in a public environment.

"I thought you said you're a pastor?" Timothy asked Jerome.

"I am."

"I thought you said your wife rides a motorcycle?" Timothy continued his line of questioning as he unabashedly gazed at Joanne's sexy outfit.

"She does."

Timothy was at a lost for words as he stared at Jerome and Joanne walking off holding hands and kissing.

"How did you get pass security?" Jerome asked Joanne.

"I know people."

Chapter Eight

Submission

"Has anyone noticed how Travis has been trying to get next to Evelyn?" Quincy Salt asked. He was in the car with his wife, La-Sondra, and their friends and neighbors, Aaron and Tonya Miller, as the four of them drove to church for Wednesday night Bible study.

"I think he's going to win her over," Tonya speculated.

"No way! She's out of his league. A woman like that is not going to give a man like Travis the time of day," Quincy announced.

"A woman like that; what do you mean mister?" La-Sondra asked.

"People normally date within their own class. Look at Travis; he's a basic, humdrum type of guy, though he is a good person. I really like the way he bounced back after losing his wife and job and raising their children. But look at him, he has a high school diploma and he's a janitor. He dresses very simple and basic, as well as his children; even his home is basic. He could never measure up to Evelyn's standards. She has a Master or a Doctoral degree, she wears the best of clothes and jewelry, lives in a nice home, has men with all type of money, education, and power chasing her, and she works with doctors all day," Quincy elaborated.

"And a white female like that with good looks, educated, has money, she's probably accustomed to dating baller or thugs like Carroll. You know they dated for a short while," Aaron added.

"You men are dumb, truly dumb. A lady wants a man who treats her like a queen, is attentive to her every need, loves and protects her, and one who goes to church. Travis seems like the man who can provide all of that," said Tonya.

"I agree," La-Sondra affirmed as she slapped Tonya a high-five.

"Ladies, Travis is a good man. His wife left him four years ago..." Quincy announced as Aaron interrupted.

"Rumor is she's dead and that she had been cheating on him for years with Carroll."

"We know the rumors. But as I was saying, he has two children, 8 and 10 years old. He purchased a small and cheap home and has since, added three additional bedrooms, a large family room, and a two-car garage. He also started his own janitor and handyman business and supports the church at all times. No matter what's going on, you can be assured Travis and his two children will be at church. Most ladies would love that type of man. You ladies are a little materialistic as well. You want a man who can provide possessions acquired with money. And I don't see it from Travis," said Quincy.

"He would be a fool to try to date her after all the rumors that not only is Carroll still interested in her, but he had something to do with Travis's wife vanishing a few years ago. I would hate to think that after all of this, Carroll and Travis would be in love with the same woman," Aaron expressed. Aaron was a police officer in Jacksonville, Florida.

"Some similar rumors are floating around in the jail and courts, such as Carroll and Krystal were seeing each other while she was with Travis," Quincy revealed. Quincy was a Corporal at Jacksonville Sheriff's office.

"Well I just hope that Travis is the winner this time. We're late. Bible study already started," said La-Sondra.

"So what do you all think about Lori and Kalevi?" Aaron inquired.

"Hmm, the jury is still out on that one," La-Sondra replied.

"Agreed," Quincy and Tonya said simultaneously.

"Does anyone know their history? I know he's been over her house doing a lot of work around the place, mostly yard work, as well as her mother's home," Tonya shared.

"Kalevi, was one of those computer geeks in high school. He and Lori dated in high school; after high school, he went into the Marine Corps. Some years later, he returned home. Sadly, he's homeless and has been living on the streets, and is unable to function in society," Quincy communicated.

"What happened in the military?" Tonya asked.

"Either no one knows or no one is talking about it," replied Quincy

"Ask the first lady. They talk every Sunday," Aaron suggested.

"And she hugs him - yuck! I know she burns her clothes when she gets home." La-Sondra scorned, causing everyone in the car to laugh.

"So what about Sofia and Coleen?" Tonya spat out.

"I don't know; I'm puzzled on that one. Those two are out of control," Quincy responded.

"Why do you say that?" La-Sondra asked.

"They're all in the open, hiding nothing. The first lady is only giving them enough rope to hang themselves. Trust me, she's going to handle it; I promise you that," Tonya declared.

"Yeah, they are wild – church girls gone wild," Aaron said as a joke.

Parking the car on the street, since the church's lot was full, the couples walked into the church and took a seat.

"Do you all think that other churches have as much drama as this Church?" asked Tonya

"Yes or more," La-Sondra responded as Quincy and Aaron agreed using body language.

"Look at Travis, he has dreams," Quincy acknowledged.

Travis and his two children were sitting on the same pew bench with Evelyn and her son. Three benches behind them were Kalevi with a bench to himself as always. On one end of the church was Sofia and on the other far end was Coleen. They were the best of friends, but acted as if they're not. It was something Demetrius taught them to help them with their hustling business.

"Last, we focus on not being revengeful, but turning the other cheek as stated in Matthew 5:39. Does anyone have any questions from last week's lesson?" Joanne asked then paused but there weren't any. Joanne was dressed in a purple, short sleeve dress that barely covered her knees. She was dressed for office work or cocktail hour with her hair pulled back in a ponytail. Her appearance was casual yet sexy.

"Okay, today's lesson is on submission. When you think of submission, what scriptures come to mind?" Joanne asked the congregation as she walked around the easel with a marker in her hand.

"Submit yourselves therefore to God. Resist the devil, and he will flee from you," Brenda yelled out as if she was talking directly to Joanne.

"James 4:7," Joanne replied as she wrote the scripture on the white paper then asked for more.

"Ephesians 5:21," Coleen shouted.

"Submitting yourselves one to another in the fear of God," Joanne replied as she jotted the scripture on the easel paper. She said, "More please."

"Ephesians 5:22," Sofia called out.

"Wives, submit yourselves unto your own husbands, as unto the Lord," Joanne replied as she added the scripture with the other two. "More please," she asked again. The church got quiet and no one responded. After a minute, Joanne walked to the easel and said, "Please write these scriptures down:

Romans 13:1–Let every soul be subject unto the higher powers. For there is no power but of God. The powers that be are ordained of God.

John 4:24–God is a Spirit: and they that worship him must worship him in spirit and in truth.

I Peter 2:13–Submit yourselves to every ordinance of man for the Lord's sake: whether it be to the king, as supreme.

I Corinthians 11:2–Now I praise you, brethren that ye remember me in all things, and keep the ordinances, as I delivered to you.

John 14:15–If ye love me, keep my commandments.

John 3:16–For God so loved the world, that he gave his only begotten Son, that whosoever believeth in him should not perish, but have everlasting life.

I think that's enough written scriptures unless someone would like to add more," Joanne invited.

Determining to continue with reading scriptures, Joanne asked the bible study members, "Can I get a volunteer to read Mathew 5:39-41, please."

A woman in the sanctuary stood up to read. "Matthew 5:39–41; I'm reading from the King James version.' And if any man will sue thee at the law, and take away thy coat, let him have thy cloak also. And whosoever shall compel thee to go a mile, go with him twain'."

"Thank you, when you read those two chapters, what comes to your mind?" Joanne inquired.

The sanctuary was full just like last week, and just like last week, the people knew Joanne was going to surprise everyone as she did with her contemplation and discernment of turning the other cheek.

Travis McKnight stood up and proclaimed, "Well, when Pastor Hill was here, he said these scriptures were the ones that Jesus used to teach on suffering for the kingdom of God."

The attendees marveled at Travis' boldness, wondering if that was what Joanne was waiting to hear. Pastor Hill was the last pastor at Abundant Truth Baptist Church before the church selected Pastor McCoy as the new pastor.

"Thank you, that's very good. Would anyone else like to add to it?" Joanne interjected.

"Jesus is teaching us to love our enemies," Brenda added.

"That's very good as well. Anyone else?" Joanne asked.

The church was quiet.

"Today's lesson is on submission. Jesus used the scripture of Mathew 5:39-41 to teach against that of the scribes and Pharisees. They taught the spirit of revenge from the Old Testament, 'Eye for eye, tooth for tooth, hand for hand, foot for foot,' Exodus 21:24. However, Jesus says that we are to resist evil. The Lord Jesus is using this example to correct the perverted teaching of the scribes and Pharisees regarding revenge."

"To understand what Jesus is talking about, we have to understand the history of the times and place where the Lord Jesus spoke in the context applicable to that particular period. Jesus spoke of a Persian's custom adopted by the Roman soldiers when traveling. They forced a person to serve as a baggage-carrier or as a guide to direct the traveler. It was the custom of that chronological timeline to demand that an individual to do this for one mile. The Lord Jesus says that if they compel you to go one mile, offer to go two miles. Why? The Jews grumbled and felt frustrated within their hearts when a Roman soldier ordered them to carry his baggage for one mile. Jesus is showing them that they had the wrong attitude and an unChristian spirit. They were not fulfilling the spirit of the law."

"One thousand paces were considered to be one mile at that time. This meant that a Roman soldier who was traveling could compel any Jew to pick up his baggage and carry it for him for one mile or one thousand paces. The Jews were extremely resentful and I think some were killed. They would count to one thousand and then refused to carry it over the mandatory one thousand paces. They would never go one step beyond what they were compelled to do. Very grudgingly, after carrying this burden one mile or one thousand paces, they set the burden down. However, the Roman soldier could command that another individual carry it for the next mile."

"We read an example of this custom in Mark 15:21, 'And they compel one Simon a Cyrenian, who passed by, coming out of the country, the father of Alexander and Rufus, to bear his cross.' The man was coming out of the country, into the city, and they arbitrarily summoned him and forced him to carry the cross. This spirit of resentment brought about much murmuring. The Jews hated the presence of the Romans in their country. It was especially humiliating for them to be driven into servitude as a baggage handler for the Romans. A Jew, regardless of his position in the community, could be forced to turn from his journey to be a servant of the Roman soldier. Wherever they were going, scribes, Pharisees, or the ordinary Jewish citizen had to alter their journey to carry a soldier's baggage."

"First Lady?" Coleen spoke.

"Yes, sister?

"So Simon, being a black man, who carried Jesus's cross, is that's why black people have so many problems in history? Are we cursed?"

"Not sure what you mean about problems or being cursed, sister."

"Slavery! I learned that blacks are cursed because a black

person carried Jesus's cross to his death, so we're cursed until Jesus returns."

Everyone was watching Joanne; they wanted to see how she would answer such a complicated question. Although Coleen was serious in her query, it was designed to confound Joanne's teaching. Joanne was pacing in front of the congregation.

"That's a really good question…good one, but let's assume that with God, nothing happens unintentionally and everything and person has a purpose. Now think about what was happening at the time." Individuals in the church were confused as to where she was going and hoping she didn't call on them. "For instance, Passover – because of the laws of Passover, carrying the cross would be unlawful for any Jew. However, the law did not apply to the Romans, nor did it apply to those from Cyrene, which is Libya today; but the law does apply to the Jews and matter to God. The Romans could have ordered anyone to carry the cross. Yet keep in mind, they wanted to keep peace in the land. The leaders of the Jews, the Sanhedrin, were needed to keep peace in the territory. For that reason, ordering a Jew to do something unlawful had the potential to cause an uproar, which would not be good for leadership. Hence, using a non-Jew was probably the right thing to do." Joanne paused and gazed at the people in the sanctuary; they looked to her as though they were pleased. "I hope I answered your question?"

Coleen was angry that Joanne provided such a great answer, but happy that she learned something new.

"What about Ham?" Sofia yelled out.

"What about him?" Joanne countered.

"Noah cursed Ham to be a servant, a slave for seeing him naked," Sofia expounded.

"And I am assuming you saying that to say Ham is the father of the black race?" Joanne said as she paced the floor slowly while thinking.

The congregants began to whisper to each other. Everyone knew the story of the curse. They anxiously awaited Joanne's response. She recognized the question was a trap. Therefore, she paused.

"That question needs a dedicated Wednesday night Bible study. But read Numbers 14:18, and Exodus 20:5. The scripture tells us that the Lord will curse to the 3rd and 4th generation. If you count the generations since Ham, the 3rd and 4th generation ended before the New Testament. Another question?"

No one said a word – the church was quiet.

"The teachings of the scribes and Pharisees were revenge, i.e., eye for eye and tooth for tooth. The Lord Jesus was showing them that they were missing the spirit of the law."

"The Lord placed the woman under the authority of her husband as a curse for rebelling against the authority of the Lord. Regrettably, the Jews overlooked the lesson. Hence, the Lord placed them under the authority of the Romans. In pronouncing the curse of the broken law upon the woman the Lord said, 'I will greatly multiply thy sorrow and thy conception; in sorrow thou shalt bring forth children; and thy desire shall be to thy husband, and he shall rule over thee,' Genesis 3:16. The word 'desire' comes from the Hebrew word, 'Teshuwqah,' which means, 'A longing desire to overflow, i.e., a desire to run over.' Think of the curse of that broken law! A woman has a longing, yearning, desire to run over her husband, yet God said, '...and he shall rule over thee'

"This curse of the broken law only results in confusion until we come under the spirit of the law'... where the Spirit of the Lord is, there is liberty'–2 Corinthians 3:17 from that curse of the law because there is submission. That's why any rebellion against such authority is rebellion against the Lord. If a woman rebels against the authority of her husband, she is not rebelling against her husband; she is rebelling against the authority of the Lord. They were overlooking the fact that it was the Lord who had placed them under the authority of the

Romans as a curse for their sin of rebellion against His Lord's will. Actually, their murmuring was against the Lord."

"The Jews had been a great nation with their own king at one time. The whole world stood in awe and fear of them when they served the Lord. When the Jews and all of Israel forsook the Lord, when they became rebellious against the Lord; the Lord brought them into captivity as punishment for their rebellion against Him. They had lost sight of the fact that the Lord had placed them under the yoke of Roman authority as a curse for their rebellion against the Lord and His will."

"Jesus was teaching that their rebellion brought the curse of a confused mind filled with a wrong attitude toward the Roman yoke. Jesus was teaching the principle that where the Spirit of the Lord is, i.e., a spirit of submission, there is liberty from such confusion of mind. The spirit of the law would lead them to repenting of their rebellion against the Lord. Then they would receive the Roman's yoke as the reward for their sin; the Jews would not resist, complain, and grumble but submit. If they were compelled to go one mile, they would cheerfully go two because they would know the Lord had placed them in that position of servitude."

"This is what the Lord Jesus was speaking of when He said, 'And whosoever shall compel thee to go a mile, go with him twain,' i.e., come into subjection. Come into submission as unto the Lord. You are not rebelling against Roman soldiers; you are rebelling against the Lord. It was the Lord who placed you in servitude, and He placed you there for your rebellion."

"The Jews were so confused in their attitude toward the spirit of the law because they were suffering under the curse of Eden. They had a yearning desire to rule over the Romans, but the Lord had put the Romans in a position to rule over them. These Jews would do absolutely the minimum required. There was not a Jew who would carry baggage one pace farther than he was compelled to. They had a frustrated, resentful spirit against the Romans, and would only go as far as they were obligated."

"The Lord Jesus contrasts this spirit of rebellion with the spirit of submission, not only as unto the Romans, but as unto the Lord. The Lord Jesus is teaching that by cheerfully submitting to those whom the Lord has placed over us, we demonstrate remorse over our rebellion, which brought us into this servitude. When we go that extra mile cheerfully, it reveals a brokenness of heart; it shows a repenting spirit. It's displaying that when rebellion is broken, the curse of the law, i.e., the confusion of mind is gone."

"By volunteering to go that extra mile, we demonstrate a spirit of submission, not unto the Romans, but unto the Lord. Romans 13:1-2 tells us, 'Let every soul be subject unto the higher powers. For there is no power but of God: the powers that be are ordained of God. Whosoever therefore resisteth the power, resisteth the ordinance of God: and they that resist shall receive to themselves damnation.' The Lord is saying when we resist the power that He placed over us, we are resisting Him; we are living in rebellion. There is no submission to the taskmaster whom He placed over us to break the rebellion in our hearts."

"That's it for today. I know last week we studied verse 39, not seeking revenge and today we focused on verse 41, submission. I know that I skipped verse 40, so please study verse 40 on your own. You will be surprised what you will learn. Does anyone have questions?"

No one asked a question. However, James McDonald, Chairman of Trustees, stood up to speak.

"First, I want to say that I truly enjoyed Bible study this evening as well as last week. I gained a deeper understanding of those two verses." Everyone in the church applauded. He continued by saying, "This Saturday, starting at 7:00 a.m., there will be a team here paving the parking lot." Everyone in the church stood up and applauded. It was something the church had been working on for more than ten years.

Since 1910, the church existed at its current location and the members had been parking on dirt and gravel since then. Approximately ten years ago, the church had started trying to get the parking lot paved. In additional to the parking lot being paved, starting tomorrow, we will begin undergoing some well-overdue maintenance in the church, such as removing some of the wooden paneling from the 70's as well as some of the wallpaper in the classrooms. Also, First Lady, we have a surprise for you."

Brenda looked at her husband and Willie with a look that said she got him.

"Thank you Trustee McDonald. I'm certain the pastor will be happy to hear that."

"Please don't tell him. We want to surprise him."

"Not a problem; my lips are sealed!" Joanne vowed with her million-dollar smile.

George Logan, the City Manager and a member of the church, as well as a member of the Trustees and Board of Director spoke out. "Since we're in the midst of revealing good news, let me share as well. I know the pastor has been asking about the three abandoned homes on the block. We know they've been abandoned for more than ten years. Mercifully, the Mayor and all 19 city council members voted to give those three abandoned homes; as well as the two empty lots to the church, as long as the church does something with them within 36 months." Again, everyone jumped to their feet, applauded, and yelled Jesus Christ. Brenda was looking as if Joanne had blackmailed two more people.

When Pastor McCoy had his first meeting with the church's members, he wrote down a list of items the members were concerned about, things that needed to be accomplished immediately as a means of progressing into a current-modern age technology. The top ten things on the pastor's list were: 1) Pave the parking lot, 2) Purchase the abandoned lots, 3) Purchase the buildings on the block, 4) Remove the old wallpaper from the walls, 5) Remove wooden paneling within the church, 6) Repaint the church, 7) Place new tile in the kitchen, 8) Place new tile in the bathrooms, 9) Put new carpet in specific areas, and 10) Convert one of the storage rooms into an office for the first lady. Unfortunately, the Trustees and many of the church members had been fighting against the pastor, but now it seemed as if the pastor was receiving more support.

The first lady closed out bible study and slowly everyone departed the church to their cars.

Kalevi walked up to Joanne and gave her a hug.

"Ms. First Lady, good evening. How are you today?"

"I'm well, Kalevi. I heard some good things about you at the construction site; keep up the good work!"

"Next week we all go on payroll, a check once a week," Kalevi said as he smiled. "But we're going to lose our home; the city gave our home to the church."

"Don't worry, I'll talk to the pastor. We'll come up with something. How is the additional work going with Sister Lori?" Kalevi smiled. Joanne assumed something good was taking place; she was still unaware that they dated once. "Okay, good night, Mr. Kalevi."

"Good night, Ms. First Lady."

"Check out the player everyone," Quincy said as he pointed to Travis and his daughters walking Evelyn and her son to her car.

***

"Babe, are you surprised that James and George had a change of heart?" Brenda asked Tyrone.

"It's okay, your brother has a plan to get rid of the pastor and first lady. I'm assuming folk are realizing why keep fighting with him, especially if the first lady is pulling everybody's string. Honesty, I think your brother's plans will fail, but I'm onboard with it."

"Really."

"On a different note, is your brother, Carroll, and Evelyn still dating?"

"No, she wants nothing to do with him. I told him to move on because he's making a fool of himself."

"You know there are still rumors about him and Krystal, Travis's wife?"

"Well I have nothing to say on that matter. She knew he was a dog. I hope she's okay wherever she may be."

Brenda and Travis continued driving home in their Ford Taurus sedan.

****

Evelyn and her son, Jason, got into their car, a Volvo XC70, and departed the church parking lot. They decided to take a slow ride home. They drove east on Kings Road, made a left turn onto N. Main street, then continued for the next 7.5 miles to W. 68th street. They made a left on W. 68th street then a quick right turn on N. Laura Street. Evelyn exited her car. As she was walking around to help her son, she heard a voice in the dark.

"Hey baby, how was your Bible study tonight?" Evelyn jumped with fear; she heard a familiar voice, but couldn't see anyone.

"No reason to fear baby, it's your man here waiting on you," Carroll said as he walked from the dark and into the light with roses in one hand and a wrapped gift in the other hand. Evelyn relaxed somewhat even though she was afraid of Carroll and confused by his actions. Carroll had been the perfect man toward Evelyn and her son; he had given her more than any woman could ask for. Evelyn loved Carroll for that, but after learning about his thuggish past, she realized it was unhealthy for her and her son to associate with him. She had asked him a million times to leave her and her son alone, but Carroll refused to accept no. He was in love with Evelyn and would do anything to have her.

"Aren't you happy to see me?"

Evelyn was quiet and didn't respond to Carroll's advances, as she continued getting her son from the car. She and her son were approaching the entrance of their home while Carroll walked behind them, still talking.

"Babe, talk to me. You know I love you and will do anything for you and your son."

Evelyn and Jason reached the front door to their home, unlocked it, and then walked in. As she closed the door, Carroll placed his foot in the doorway, stopping it from closing. Evelyn was really frightened by his action.

"Why won't you talk to me?"

"I've asked you nicely to leave me and my son alone. Please don't come over here again or call my home, cell, or work numbers, please."

"What did I do wrong? I think I deserve an answer."

"Goodbye!" Evelyn snapped and harshly shut the door. Then she quickly stood by the door and peeked through the keyhole to see what Carroll was doing. He placed the roses and wrapped gift at the front door, slowly turned around, and walked to his car and then left.

****

Joanne parked her motorcycle in the parking lot of Applebee's on a sunny Thursday afternoon. She was there to meet Evelyn for lunch. She walked into the restaurant and saw Evelyn at a booth, then walked over and sat down. It was the afternoon after Carroll's surprise visit the previous evening. Now that the pastor had agreed to compete in the Ironman

Triathlon with Jason, Evelyn assumed it was time for her and Joanne to have a one-on-one to get to know each other better.

"Good afternoon, how are?" Joanne asked Evelyn.

"I'm well. I'm glad you were able to meet on such short notice."

"Not a problem. What can I do for you?"

"I ordered us a few appetizers. I hope that's fine with you," Evelyn informed her.

"It is. Thank you."

The waitress brought the appetizers, two glasses of water, and two plates to the table. Then the ladies blessed the food.

Evelyn started the conversation by saying; "First, I really want to thank you and the pastor for what he's doing with my son. It means so much to both him and I."

"You're welcome. That's just the type of person the pastor is," said Joanne, knowing David had tricked him into it.

"Well it means so much to Jason. I'm extremely grateful and happy."

Joanne was confused. She kept asking herself what this woman wanted to meet about and what was hot on her mind.

"Not a problem. Is there anything else you would like to talk about?"

"Yes, do you know a Carroll Benson?" Evelyn asked.

"No, should I?"

"No, not really. He's a man I dated a few years ago, a very nice and handsome man. He treated my son and I with the utmost respect. I really thought I had found my knight in shining armor coming to rescue me."

"Sounds great but I'm assuming you two are no longer dating?"

Evelyn responded, "No, it lasted about three months and then I ended it. However, he keeps calling my home, cell, and work number; as well as coming to my home as he did last night. This was the first time he really scared me – he placed his foot in my doorway, told me that he loved me, and wanted me in his life."

"And?"

"I love him. Well I thought I loved him. He has an ugly past, a very ugly past. But you know some people never change."

"Okay, you have my attention," Joanne replied.

"Carroll is a rich and very successful man in the Jacksonville area. Rumor has it that the money he made from selling drugs and other illegal activities, was what he used to invest in his legal business today. I accepted that, he broke the law, he served his time, and is now a successful business man."

"But?"

"But, some people never change. One day I was at Carroll's home and he cooked a really nice dinner. While I offered to prepare dessert in his kitchen, I came across a large stash of cash under the kitchen sink, and two guns as well as a gun in the refrigerator. Even though I knew it wasn't the norm, I overlooked it and moved on. That same night, two women and a man came to visit him, but didn't come inside. Instead, they walked around the outside of the house to the patio in the back. While in the kitchen cleaning, I could hear them talking about a dead body. They mentioned the mayor and police chief's names a few times and an investigation of someone or something."

"Wow, that is deep!" Joanne replied as she listened intently to hear more drama.

"It gets deeper. The next day while at work, I was talking to a police officer friend, Walter Don, about any recent killings and or bodies missing or large investigations. He told me about a Krystal McKnight, the wife of Travis McKnight. At the time, I didn't know Travis. I met Travis about a year ago after joining Abundant Truth Baptist Church and that conversation took place about three years before I met Travis. Krystal's family was convinced Carroll had something to do with her missing. However, Carroll had information on the mayor and police chief that prevented them from investigating him."

"Have you told anyone about this?"

"No."

Joanne was confused now and wondering why she was telling her.

"So what do you want to do about it?"

"I received this text message today." Evelyn showed it to Joanne – *"You will be with me or no one."*

"OMG, who is this from?"

"Carroll, I'm assuming, but I can't prove it."

"What are you going to do?"

"What can I do?"

"Right."

They sat there and stared at one another.

"I need to get back to the hospital, "said Evelyn

"We must finish this conversation, but I need to get to the airport. The pastor's flight will be landing soon. He wanted me to let you know that, starting Monday, he'll be picking Jason up for training. The race is only weeks away."

"Thank you."

Joanne got up and left. She had to drive home, park her motorcycle, and get into her F-type convertible Jaguar to pick up her husband from the airport.

Evelyn returned to work.

Chapter Nine

It's Time

"This is your time Abundant Truth Baptist Church," yelled Pastor McCoy from the pulpit as he preached at the noon service.

"I have received compliments from many of you about the changes that have taken place in the last few weeks and months. Give the glory to the most high, our Father in Heaven, not to me. The scripture tells us in Ecclesiastes 3:1-9, that there is a time for everything under Heaven. A season is a certain time appointed by God for its being and continuance, which no human wit, or providence can alter. And by virtue of this appointment of God, all vicissitudes that happen in the world, whether comforts or calamities, come to pass. Which is added to prove the principal proposition, that all things below are vain, and happiness is not to be found in them because of their great uncertainty, and mutability, and transistorizes, and because they are so much out of the reach and power of men, and wholly in the disposal of God."

"Purpose - not only natural, but even the voluntary actions of men, are ordered and disposed by God. But it must be considered that here He does not speak of a time allowed by God, wherein all the following things may lawfully be done, but only of a time fixed by God, in which they are actually done," Pastor McCoy declared as he summarized Ecclesiastes 3:1-9.

Every soul in the church applauded.

"And such as it is a time for the church, it is a time for Jason Harrison. He prepared for three years to compete in the Ironman race. Though Satan tried to steal his glory, our Lord

116

in heaven has heard his prayer and released his angels to answer Jason's prayer request. Jason your time and season is now. Abundant Truth, I am here to tell you, if you were praying for a relationship, your time is now; if you were praying for financial breakthrough, your time is now. Know that our Lord in Heaven is still in the blessing business. He is still answering prayers. He is still in control and it's not your time until he says so. Do not stop believing, do not give up, but keep praying, and keep the faith. If you hear me and believe in the Lord Jesus, stand on your feet and give our Lord in Heaven some praise."

"I know Travis received that word today," Quincy said to his wife, La-Sondra.

"And Kalevi," La-Sondra added. "I wish them both the best of luck."

"That's my time." Pastor McCoy closed out the noon service with a prayer and then everyone slowly departed the church and headed home. Brenda went over to the first lady and began a conversation.

Sofia and Coleen watched the first lady talking in the sanctuary and the pastor walking to his office. Not knowing what the other was thinking, both ladies quickly made their way to the pastor's office.

"Good afternoon First Lady. How are you today?"

"Ms. Cummings, I am well, how can I help you?"

"There have been a lot of changes in the church, such as: the Culinary – a new menu, Health ministry with new ideas, the Ushers, the Trustees overseeing the paving of the parking lot and remodeling the church; such as removing the wooden paneling and wallpaper and painting the building inside and out. There is also the deacons and city manager. Remarkably, the pastor has accomplished many of these changes within months."

Joanne was confused as to where Brenda Cummings was going with the conversation. Yet, she was aware that she was walking her into a big question or problem.

"I think it's wonderful that everyone is supporting the growth of the church," Joanne responded.

"Or the vision of the pastor," Brenda replied.

"Excuse me!"

"What I mean is everyone is supporting the vision of the pastor. However, there are a few things I don't think the pastor is aware of."

"Sweetie..." Normally, Joanne didn't use words like sweetie, but it was an attempt to refrain from losing her cool. "You should tell your deacon or one of the trustees and have them bring it up in a church business meeting. What do you plan to gain by telling me?"

"Well they know, but they won't share it with the pastor."

"Really, why not?"

"Well it's the parking situation. When people park on the street and in other business parking lots, they're getting tickets, about 10 to 15 each Sunday, maybe more."

"Do they park legally?"

"No, but those businesses are closed on Sundays, and they gave us verbal permission to park on their property. Another problem is the Church Clerk. She doesn't attend the church business meetings nor does she record minutes and distribute them to the members. She also doesn't schedule appointments for the pastor, or complete other administrative duties. By the way, the broken vending machine in the building should be replaced with a healthy vending machine and we should maintain it ourselves and keep the money within the church."

"Those are all good ideas I will share with pastor, anything else?"

"No, that's all," Brenda smiled.

"Have a nice day." Joanne walked away and ran into James, Chairman of the Trustees.

Sofia reached the pastor's office. The door was partially open, so she began to walk in but someone on the other side prevented her from entering further.

"May I help you ma'am?" Kalevi asked as he extended his head between the door and doorframe, slowly positioning his entire body in the doorway.

"Kalevi, what the hell! I mean what are you doing here?" Sofia asked, as she was taken by surprised to see how attractive Kalevi is after he cleaned up and dressed in a two-piece suit.

"How may I help you?"

"I need to see the pastor please. I normally come over after he preaches to see if he needs anything."

"I need your name and the reason you need to see the pastor?"

"What! Tell him Sofia is out here, he'll let me in."

"No ma'am Ms. Sofia, you need to make an appointment to see him during ministry hours."

"Says who?"

"Ms. First Lady."

"Who are you and why are you here?"

"Kalevi Dameon Richardson, I'm the pastor's armor-bearer."

Sofia wrinkled up her nose and turned around where she observed Coleen walking toward the pastor's office with coffee and a bowl of fruit.

"Good luck," Sofia said to Coleen, who knocked on the pastor's office door.

Kalevi opened the door and asked, "May I help you ma'am?"

"I'm Sister Coleen; I have the pastor's coffee and fruit. May I come in?"

"The pastor already has his coffee and fruit."

"May I see the pastor?"

"No ma'am, you need to make an appointment during his ministry hours; call the church office."

Coleen was angry. Looking off to her side, she noticed Sofia standing there. Turning around, she walked back to the kitchen

"Ms. McCoy, how do you like your office?" asked James, Chairman of the Trustees.

"I love it! Thank you for the hard work. In fact, I like all of the work you and everyone else have been doing. It has really added beauty to the church."

"Thank you First Lady."

Sofia and Coleen were in the parking lot, walking to their cars. They slowed down as they overheard people talking.

"So what's up with Kalevi, the homeless man posted as the pastor's bodyguard?"

"It's the first lady, there have been some rumors that he's sleeping with people in the church. Now he's never alone, which makes it difficult to start rumors about him."

"Why the homeless man; is he the best the church has to offer the pastor?"

"Again, the first lady, she knows what she's doing and whom she can trust."

"Kalevi, how was your first day on the job?" Joanne inquired as she arrived at the pastor's office still talking to James.

"I'll get used to it. Thanks for the suit."

"Good."

James and Joanne walked away. Everyone departed the church except the pastor and Kalevi. Later, the two of them departed his office, turned on the alarm, and exited through the side door. As the pastor took a step, he paused as he noticed a white, Chevrolet Corvette Stingray parked behind his Chrysler 300. Pastor McCoy patiently waited as the door of the Corvette opened slowly. Kalevi recognized the car as well as the driver. Hence, he wasn't concerned; he continued to stand on the right side of Pastor McCoy.

"Pastor Doctor Jerome Samiah McCoy, from Seattle, Washington, South Seattle I presume?" Carroll said as he exited his Stingray and walked toward Pastor McCoy and Kalevi. Carroll nodded his head to Kalevi as a sign of acknowledgement as well as a greeting. Kalevi returned his nod as a matter of respect.

Carroll was 6' 1", 240 lbs, and 45 years old. His criminal activities started when he was ten years old, running errands for the local gangster, which included delivering drugs on his Schwinn ten-speed bike that he stole from the downtown area of Jacksonville. He had two older sisters, one lives in the New Haven, Connecticut and was a professor at Southern Connecticut State University, and his other sister was a Master Chief Petty Officer in the United States Navy. His mother was killed when he was five years old after a drug deal went bad. His father was serving life in prison for killing four men. Although the rumors are he killed more, it was never proven in court. The four men Carroll's father was serving time for killing are the men that killed his mother. Demetrius was partially raised by his older sisters, and grandparents. At the age of fourteen the local gangster took him in as one of his own children and raised him, which exposed him to more illegal activities, cruel treatment of rivalry gangs and non-loyalty gang members on a daily bases. By the time Demetrius turned 21, he had his own crew and conducted illegal actives from drugs, prostitution, selling of stolen items, pornography, gambling on sports, human trafficking, arms trafficking, and a list of legal actives; such as investing in the stock markets, which he maintained in the name of his two sisters. Although he served time in prison on multiple occasions, he was presently known as a legitimate businessman in Jacksonville, Florida.

"That's correct. Mr. Carroll Jordan Benson, the local thug turned business, I'm assuming?"

"I see you've heard of me."

"No, not really. I was told the 'Thug of Jacksonville' has a white car of that style. Is it true?"

"Thug of Jacksonville, cute; I own all of the Chevrolet dealerships."

"What can I do for you, sir?" Pastor McCoy asked.

"Yeah, let's get right to business. The church nor the community hates you or your wife. They just want a black pastor; and I'm sure you get that."

"We don't always get what we want, right? Even you understand that!"

"Pastor, I'm being respectful. I ask that you do the same. Please listen. The people want you to leave."

"And they voted you to be the one to deliver the message? You're asking me to do what you yourself are unwilling to do?"

"I was born and raised here, not you. This city and the people, we all have history."

"But I'm not staying where I was asked to leave and I'm not forcing myself where I have not been invited."

"Preacher, this is not your home; this is not your community. It's time for your departure."

"Mr. Benson, I will leave this church when the members ask me to go away or my Lord tells me to go. Other than that, I'll leave Jacksonville when I'm ready."

"Staying can be dangerous for your health."

"Really, my health is good. Trust me, I exercise three to four days a week."

"You're really pushing my buttons and you don't wanna do that. You talk like a black man, but you're not one of us. No matter how many black females you screw or give you a blow job, or how much fried chicken and collar greens you eat that still won't make you black," Carroll declared as he took a few steps toward Pastor McCoy in an aggressive manner.

Before Pastor McCoy could respond, a voice from a distance called out his name.

"Pastor McCoy!" Travis yelled. Carroll and Pastor McCoy turned in Travis's direction as he approached the three men. Travis then said, "Pastor, I saw your car and decided to see if you needed some help."

"We're fine. Go home," Carroll ordered Travis. With rage in their eyes, the two men stared each other down, knowing they were only delaying the inevitable – a nasty showdown that would leave one or both of them dead. Aware that the two of them were trouble, Kalevi positioned himself closer to Travis and Carroll.

Pastor McCoy noticed the fire in each man's eyes and recognized it was time to bring this unscheduled meeting to an end.

"This meeting is over, Mr. Benson! I have a dinner date with my wife. Please move your car. Travis, all is well here. Enjoy your day; please go home."

Carroll turned around, got into his car, and drove off. Then Travis walked away and Pastor McCoy got into his vehicle and drove home.

The first Lady

Pastor McCoy arrived home and picked up his wife. They drove to the Jacksonville Landing for dinner. They parked their car then proceeded from the garage in the direction of the restaurant. They were dining at Benny's Steak & Seafood. The waiter escorted them to their seats, which had a window view where they could enjoy the lights of the boats that were on the river. After being seated and handed two menus by the waiter, they placed their order and enjoyed a nice conversation. Jerome ordered Louisiana Seafood Gumbo and Spinach Salad. Joanne ordered the Chef's Specialty, Seafood Jambalaya.

"I had a visit today after service from Carroll Benson. Do you know the name?"

"He is popular. Evelyn spoke of him recently."

"Really? I would have never pictured the two of them as a couple."

"They're not a couple. He wants them to be but she's not feeling it."

"Good for her. Travis has shown great interest in her; I'm pulling for him," Jerome smiled.

"What did Carroll want?"

"He wants me to leave town?"

"And your reply?"

"I told him my wife would not allow me to leave."

Both of them smiled and then started laughing.

"I'm glad you know that."

"I got the message baby. It's surprising how everyone made changes all within a few weeks of each other. Why do you think that is?"

"Like you said today, time and season, baby, time and season."

Jerome smiled.

"Okay, that's good for me. I never knew a pastor would have so much drama to deal with at a church."

"Drama! Is there more besides the anonymous ladies wanting you?"

"Drama! People in the church vote me to be the pastor and then fight against my vision; the rumors of me cheating on my wife; and yes, the nameless messages and images of females' private parts; the tricks, and the local thug. Helping the homeless, I'm okay with that. The rest is drama, too much drama."

"Write a book. Title it, The Drama of a Pastor." Joanne and Jerome chuckled. "Are you ready for the race?" Joanne asked.

"Yes, I am. I doubt if I'll do all 72.3 miles, but I am feeling good."

"Evelyn is very excited. Three weeks before your big day. It's coming soon, pastor."

"I'm telling you now, have a stretcher and oxygen at the finish line. I'm leaving all that I have on the street."

Continuing their conversation, Jerome and Joanne enjoyed their dinner date.

****

Tuesday, at 6:30 a.m. with light rain dropping on Joanne's car, Joanne got out of her bed and walked to the kitchen to start a pot of coffee. She returned to her bedroom to enjoy a nice hot shower. After her shower, she applied lotion to her nude body. Then she walked in front of her husband and handed him the bottle of lotion so he could lotion her backside. Afterwards, Joanne put on her cream-colored, satin bathrobe and went into the kitchen to prepare two cups of coffee. Returning to the master bedroom, she gave one of the cups to her husband.

"Thank you. What time is your appointment today?"

"You're welcome. My first one is at 9:00 a.m. at The Plaza Ocean Club in Daytona Beach. Then I have an appointment on the Southside at 2:00 p.m. What are you doing today?"

"The big race is two weeks away, so I'm still conditioning for it."

"So what else has David volunteered you for?"

"We can talk about it another day. You need to be going so you're not late."

Joanne finished getting dressed, kissed her husband, walked out of her house, and got into her car. She drove south on I-95 to her designation, The Plaza Ocean Club. While driving, Joanne called her mother and enjoyed an early morning conversation with her best friend. As she arrived to her destination she parked her car, she entered the lobby of the hotel where the hotel manager, Susan Hunt, was waiting for her.

"Joanne McCoy," Susan greeted as she extended her hand to shake hands with a warm, welcoming smile.

"Yes. I'm assuming you're Susan, Susan Hunt."

"Yes I am. Can I get you something to drink?"

"No thank you, I would like to start with a tour of the hotel please."

"Okay, the hotel has eight levels and 900 rooms. Let's get started."

Joanne and Susan embarked on a detailed and full tour of the hotel. As they arrived on the 7th floor and walked down the hall, a happy and playful couple exited the room laughing and playing. They accidentally ran into Joanne.

"Oh excuse me," Karen and Danny said simultaneously. Quickly, Karen realized she had bumped into Joanne McCoy, the First Lady of Abundant Truth Baptist Church, where she's a member and president of the music ministry. Accompanying her was Danny Salesman, a Lieutenant with the Jacksonville Police Department. Without thinking, Joanne and Susan started walking with Danny and Karen in the opposite direction.

Karen was tall and thin, pretty in the face with long hair, but had no curves to her body. She was a local elementary schoolteacher and very active in the local political world and well known and liked in the community as well as the church. Danny was an arrogant police officer, with the city of Jacksonville; he served three years in the U.S. Marine Corp, and still maintained the high and tight marine haircut. He also acted as if he and all police officers were on active military duty. He looked up to the Mayor as a positive role model, not knowing that the Mayor was once part of Carroll's crew. He did not like Carroll, but learned to stay out of his path.

"I'm surprised to see you two here of all places. How are you both doing today?"

Karen and Danny were quiet; they didn't reply to Joanne's question. At the moment, they were not in a good predicament. Karen, as well as Danny, were married. Unfortunately, not to each other and they knew Joanne was aware of this. Thus, they quietly walked down the hall.

Tasha, the hotel housekeeper, walked out of the room that Danny and Karen had exited. Tasha was on her cell phone talking very loudly to Darcy, the hotel front desk clerk.

"Darcy girl, the people that just came out of room 1243 are some freaks! Make sure you take a very good look at them," Tasha exclaimed. She was speaking so loudly that Joanne, Susan, Danny, and Karen could clearly hear her. "Girl, there are about a dozen or more salami slings in the trash can and a bottle of Pjur Back Door and a bottle of Maximus lubricant. You know what that's for – backdoor action!"

"Excuse me." Stepping away from the group, Susan walked down the hallway to quiet Tasha from further embarrassing the hotel guests.

Danny, Karen, and Joanne conversed briefly, and then Joanne rejoined Susan so they could finish their tour. Danny and Karen stepped onto the elevator and took it to the lobby. They checked out of their room at the front desk and continued to their car without saying a word to each other. They had known each other all of their lives; they grew up going to the same elementary, middle, and high school. Approximately 10 years ago, they engaged in an extramarital affair and began seeing each other one to three times a month, meeting at various places in and out of the city.

"What do you think of that?" Karen finally asked Danny.

"What?"

"Us running into her."

"Ah, though it's a little bit of a shock, there's no reason to panic."

"Wrong answer, start panicking. I heard about her. She's been blackmailing people in the church in order to get them to do what the pastor wants."

"I heard; and it's not blackmail, it's paranoia," Danny retorted.

"Whatever. You need to go upstairs and get the trash from our room."

"There you go; you're paranoid. What do you think she can blackmail you or I over?"

"News flash, for starters, she knows we're both married and not to each other."

"So what? If she gets into my business, she'll regret it. I don't scare that easy."

"Will you stop being so dumb and macho? Do you want a divorce? Not me. Do you want your name tarnished on the

128

force as being an adulterer? Not me. Do you want to explain this to your children? Not me. Now go get the trash; those condoms, lubricants, and bottles of wines! Those things place our DNA together and that's all the proof she needs to get us busted. Please go now!" Karen demanded in a loud and fearful voice.

"Trust me, she has nothing. In a few days, I'll visit her in my uniform, so don't worry."

"Listen, from what I heard, a lady like that is not afraid of you or your police uniform. Now please get out of the car and go get the trash from our room. Now please!

Reluctantly, Danny returned to the 7th floor. He saw Tasha, the housekeeper, and walked up to her.

"Ma'am, I'd like to get the trash from room 1243 if possible," Danny said as he handed Tasha a fifty-dollar bill.

"Keep your money. You're free to look for it." Tasha wanted the money, but employees had been fired for such things. It was called selling items that belonged to the hotel and she didn't know if it was a setup or not. Therefore, she went into the next room and started cleaning as usual. Danny was going through the trash, but was unable to locate the items from his room.

"Excuse me. Have you dumped your trash since you cleaned room 1243?"

"No sir."

"Has anyone been around your trash since you cleaned 1243?"

"Just the manager and her guest."

Danny called Karen on the cell phone and yelled, "The trash is gone!"

"What? She has it! You need to get it back before she leaves the hotel. Wait, I see her walking to her car."

Joanne gets into her car and calls her mother.

"Yes dear."

"I hope you are sitting down, this is going to shock you big time and I do mean big time."

"Does she have a trash bag with her?"

"No."

Danny returned to the car where Karen was waiting on him. As they drove back to Jacksonville, Karen sent an email and a text message to the members of the church choir.

****

"Good evening everyone. I'm assuming you all received my text message today, so you all know we have a lot to do. So please get in your positions because we'll be learning new songs tonight," said Karen, the head of the Ministry of Music at Abundant Truth Baptist Church. Karen then said, "As you all know, Pastor McCoy has requested that we sing more modern songs as well as create a three to five person group to be the praise and worship team."

It was 7:00 p.m. on Thursday night, time for the Abundant Truth Baptist Church mass choir rehearsal. The church had three choirs – a mass choir, a male choir, and a youth choir. Karen managed all three of them. Once a year, the ladies came together to form a choir to sing on Women's Day.

One of the things church visitors and members had been complaining about was church services started slowly, and people were normally in the church for a half-hour to forty-five minutes before they got into the spirit. Pastor McCoy requested that a praise team be implemented for the purpose of getting people in the spirit as soon as they entered the church. The praise team would start fifteen minutes prior to the beginning of service and would consist of singing, praying, and testimonials. Karen refused to execute the pastor's vision. She felt it wasn't needed; the traditional way of doing things had been working for the church and there was no need for change, such as singing more current songs. On the contrary, now Karen had to please Joanne and the pastor. Consequently out of fear and the unknown, she was forced to comply with their wishes.

"Why the change all of a sudden?" a member of the choir asked.

"I'm embracing the pastor's vision, and as long as I'm the Minister of Music, we will support the pastor's ideas."

"I agree. It's just that it conflicts with what you've been saying for months."

"Well I'm onboard now. Would anyone like to volunteer to be on the praise team?"

"Karen, is the pastor going to do anything about those parking tickets? The church keeps growing and parking spaces are tight. The business across the street is closed on Sundays and gave us permission to use their parking lot, but Jacksonville's finest have been writing tickets."

Karen quickly recalled her and Danny running into Joanne McCoy at the hotel. She knew that the police officers that patrol the area around the church were under Danny's supervision. She thought to herself, dammit, she got us both. Speaking so everyone could hear her, she speculated, "I don't know if anyone talked to the pastor or not, but something tells me that Jacksonville's finest have written their last tickets, at least when Abundant Truth Baptist Church is having service."

****

It was Saturday morning, Pastor McCoy had arranged for the culinary ministry to provide a breakfast for a special meeting in the dining area of the church for approximately thirty people. The meeting was about the Ironman race scheduled to take place the following week with Pastor McCoy and Jason Harrison. The meeting had been in session for half an hour now and Calvin was speaking.

"It's imperative that you be on time and at your designated station. As soon as the pastor and Jason reaches you, you'll give them their banana or sandwich then you have to rush to your next appointed post. Like the pastor said, 'He's leaving it all on the track,' so it's important that you're there. We have two jogger wheelchairs, one inflatable rubber boat, and two wheelchair bicycles. As I said, the early part of the race involves jogging, swimming, and bicycling three times. So after the first time, you must reposition the equipment. Even though you can assist with the equipment, you cannot touch the runners. They, of course, are pastor and Jason. If you touch either of them, it's considered assisting the runner and they'll be disqualified. However, you are allowed to handle the wheelchair, bicycle, and boat."

"Brother Calvin, I don't want to sound negative, but is this a promotional stunt? I mean what makes the pastor think he can win? I mean it's not like this is a marathon or a half marathon; this is an Ironman race–running, bike riding and swimming."

The pastor stood up to speak. His response was, "Well this is a first for me, but I've played sports all of my life…" Before he could say another word, Evelyn stood up.

"Excuse me Pastor McCoy, may I?" Pastor McCoy nodded his head in affirmation. "My son, Jason, dedicated two years to conditioning himself for this race. You must be 18 years old to enter. Four months before his 18th birthday, and six months before the race, he received a flu shot. He was disabled as a result of that injection. He still talks and writes about competing in the Ironman race and as a mother it hurts. I am a victim of rape, so my son doesn't have a father that he can call daddy. On numerous occasions, I have asked men within the church and other big brother programs in the area if someone would enter the race with him. Winning is good, but just being in the race is a dream come true for him. So I'm happy Pastor McCoy is here as pastor and that he volunteered to do this race with my son."

Calvin looked at David and smiled; the room was so quiet, you could hear a pin drop.

"Does anyone else have a question?"

No one replied. "I'll have my cell phone with me, so if you have any questions at any time, please do not hesitate to call me."

Calvin closed out the meeting with a prayer. Slowly, everyone exited the dining area and church. Coleen walked up to Evelyn and Sofia walked up to Calvin.

"I think that's a wonderful thing the pastor is doing for your son. What is he doing for you?"

"Excuse me?"

"Sister, we all know what's going on. You want us to think the pastor is running 72.3 miles for a handicapped child and getting nothing in return." Coleen put on a faux smile so people would get the impression they were having an enjoyable conversation.

"Have a nice day," Was Evelyn's response as she turned around and walked away.

"Brother Calvin, I'm the pastor's nurse; where do you need me for the race?"

"Nurse, I didn't know he had one."

"Yes, it's me."

"Well you can be at the finish line with me and the First Lady."

"The First Lady! Why is she going to be there? It's not like she's in the race."

"Moral support I assume. Many people will be there that aren't in the race. Have a nice day, bye," Calvin said as he walked away, shaking his head and thinking that was an odd conversation.

Chapter Ten

The Clerk

Sharon Macy, the church clerk for Abundant Truth Baptist Church, was with her husband, Leroy Macy. They were on Arlington Expressway driving to the Target located next to Regency Square Mall on a Thursday afternoon.

Sharon lived a very basic lifestyle, as the only child and raised by a single parent, her mother raised her to be the prefect mother and wife. At the age of 42, she'd never received a parking or speed ticket, only attended concerts and events with a biblical reference, never had a drink of alcohol. Her mother was not happy when she learned that her only daughter would marry Leroy. She was priming her daughter to be the wife of a Pastor, CEO, political figure; not a barber, but she accepted Leroy, because that is who her daughter loved.

"Do you find it odd that everyone is slowly changing their opposition to now supporting the pastor's vision?" Sharon asked Leroy.

"Not sure what you mean."

"Think about it. The pastor asked each ministry to make some changes, and for a lack of better words, each ministry told him to suck an egg. However, each one of them eventually had a change of heart, as if someone was coercing them."

"I think they're realizing that it's more beneficial for the church to support the pastor, but Christian Education hasn't made any changes to their ministry."

"Many of us, me included, agreed to give him a hard time so he would leave. Those very same individuals are changing their minds out of the blue and now are in harmony with his vision. Furthermore, Christian Education never opposed the Pastor's vision."

"Well, personally, I think the whole idea of going against him was stupid and sad. I like the pastor; I think he's a good teacher and preacher," Leroy commented.

"It is strange. Last week, my brother, Eric, told me that their lieutenant, Danny Salesman, instructed them not to write any more tickets while people are parked to attend church service on Sundays. He even changed his position, why?" Sharon asked.

"Maybe he realized he and Karen aren't the only ones who know about their private getaways," Leroy suggested.

"You have an answer for everything, you know that?"

"No, I don't. I'm just sharing facts, baby. Not everyone has facts. Most people base their conversation on theories and rumors. What are you going to do when it's your turn to change?"

"I'm a child of the Most High. I have no dark secrets or skeletons in my closet, so trust me, they cannot get to me. On the other hand, Brenda has a very good theory about it all."

The Macys parked in the Target store parking lot, and then exited the car and entered the store. After walking up and down a few aisles, Sharon spotted Joanne and quickly went to speak to her.

"Good afternoon Joanne; how are you?" Sharon greeted.

"Good afternoon to you; I'm well."

"Can we sit and talk, please?"

Joanne smiled, "Not a problem. Now or later?"

"Now please, there are some empty seats at Starbucks."

They proceeded to the Starbucks inside Target and sat in the corner.

"Joanne, I don't know how much you've learned over the past few months, but a shift has been taking place in the church..."

"For the better I hope?" Joanne quickly interjected.

"Well, time will tell. There's been a shift from people staunchly being unsupportive to delightfully promoting the pastor's vision is what I want to discuss."

"I'm assuming that's a good thing." Joanne responded.

"Well, has anyone asked why these people have changed their minds? Do they earnestly believe it's the right thing to do or are they being blackmailed?"

"Has anyone asked the individuals themselves?" Joanne questioned.

"No, not to my knowledge."

"I would say that would be a start. Then again, I'm presupposing that rallying around the pastor's direction is an affirmation of progress. What do you think?"

"I'm not sure; is that scripture?"

"Scripture! The question I'm asking is the same one the pastor asked. Is that what's making people rebel against him?"

Sharon was thrown off-guard. Along with everyone else, she recognized that the direction the pastor wanted to move in was valuable for the members, the community, as well as the growth of the church. Clearly, she couldn't reveal the real reason people were working against the pastor.

"Well I am the church clerk and have been for the past five years and I do my job well. Since Pastor McCoy has been here, he wants me, the clerk, to attend all church board meetings and business meetings to record minutes. I also have to prepare agendas for church meetings with his assistance, and then the board chairman will distribute the minutes of previous board meetings along with the agenda to the board members before the next meeting."

"Additional duties include maintaining minutes from board meetings and business meetings; as well as attending statewide clerk conferences. Maybe it also consists of being a permanent member of the Church Board and Trustees, plus creating quarterly newsletters for church members."

"Joanne, for the past five years, all I was required to do was monthly finance records, report to the pastor who was not paying their tithes, and schedule his appointments outside of the church. Now I'm sure you would agree that's a big shift in my duties as church clerk. Plus, he's telling me to stop reporting to him who pays their tithes. He claims that offerings and tithes is a personal relationship between the individual and the Lord. I talked to my other pastor friends and they claim he's full of bull. They believe all pastors want to know which members are not paying their tithes, but not Pastor Jerome McCoy!"

"I'm not sure what you want me to say. However, no one should be in a non-paying position for five years. Who decides the duties and responsibilities of the church clerk?"

"I'm just saying, you would agree that Pastor McCoy is placing a tremendous amount of work on me as the clerk, compared to what was required of me for the past five years. I am not doing it! They can remove me from the position; I will not perform all the duties he's asking of me as clerk. After all, it's not like my position is a paid position. Well, they do give me a little something the first of each month, $200."

"Sharon…" Joanne started, but before Joanne could say another word, Sharon's husband walked up.

"Excuse me ladies," Leroy said as he looked at his wife. He then said, "I'll be outside when you're ready. Take your time." Leroy turned around and began to walk away with shopping bags in his hands.

"Leroy, Demetrius Watson told me to tell you hi." Leroy's heart dropped down to his shoes. Sharon was not happy to hear the name Demetrius. "Demetrius is my hairstylist; he said he knows you and your family and wanted me to tell you hi."

"Thank you," Leroy replied in an indifferent manner as he calmly walked away, realizing the ride home with his wife would not be a good one.

Demetrius was the owner of four, high-class salons in the Jacksonville, Florida area, and was known as the best hairstylist in the region as well. He was a bodybuilder, held the rank of ninth dan in Judo, and stood at 6'1", weighing in at 225 pounds. Demetrius was openly gay. Anyone who knew him knew he was gay.

Leroy owned a local barbershop on Kings Road. He had been in the business all of his life. It was a trade he learned from his father and grandfather. His grandfather started the shop he presently occupied.

About seven years prior, Demetrius and Leroy ventured into a joint business. The plan was that Demetrius would be the hairstylist for the ladies and Leroy would groom the men. The business started out well; every day the place was full of customers. One day, when Sharon was heading home from a night of shopping for Christmas gifts, she decided to stop by the shop. The lights were off as if the business was closed for the day. Sharon walked around back and noticed the back door was not completely shut. She was able to see that the light in the back room was on as well.

As she got closer, she could hear music and a song she had never heard before. Later she learned the name of the song was "Love To Be Loved." Sharon walked inside the shop from the back door and noticed her husband, Leroy Macy, and his business partner, Demetrius Watson, kissing each other with their shirts off. Yelling out to her husband, she caused the two to stop kissing and they quickly got dressed. Sharon ran out and went home. Sharon and Leroy managed to keep their marriage together. Leroy claimed that the incident was a one time experience and would never happen again. Almost seven years later, a name from their dark past had resurfaced. Sharon was not happy.

"What I was getting ready to say…"

"I need to go! My man is waiting on me. I need to go. Have a good day," Sharon said as she hurriedly got up and went to meet her husband. They looked at each other. Without speaking a word, both of them walked to their car and started their return trip home.

"So what do you think? Do you think she knows about your gay experience?"

Because of her choice of words – gay experience, Leroy looked at his wife strangely.

"Who knows what she knows and we shouldn't care."

"So what do we do now?"

"Nothing, just keep living our lives."

"Really, and you think she'll keep quiet?"

"What does she know, Sharon, huh?"

"She knows Demetrius."

"Almost every female and gay person in the area knows him and he is gay. Can you please relax and just live your life? Don't even worry about that."

"Leroy, he knows your home and work location. If he wanted to say hi, he could call you at work or home or stop by your shop. Why is it coming from her?"

"Babe, please relax and leave it."

"Men! I truly hope you all aren't a true image of the Lord Jesus."

"What?"

"She's playing you. She mentioned Demetrius at the perfect time. She patiently waited for your arrival to catch you off-guard, off your game, and watch your reaction when his name was mentioned. She knows. Trust me, she knows about your experience and who knows what Demetrius told her you two did together."

Leroy remained quiet as the couple continued their drive home. Unbeknownst to Sharon, Demetrius and Leroy never stopped seeing each other or enjoying one another's company.

****

Pastor McCoy had just concluded Wednesday night Bible study and asked if anyone had an announcement to make. Sharon Macy stood up.

"Good evening everyone. I want to follow up on an email I sent out pertaining to the duties of the church clerk. Effective immediately, I will be attending all church meetings to record minutes. For that reason, please let me know the dates and times of your ministry meetings so that I can update the church calendar. With the assistance of the pastor and board chairman, I will also start preparing agendas for church board meetings. Before the next meeting, I will distribute minutes from previous board meetings, along with the agenda to all board members. In addition, I will maintain board meetings, as well as business meeting records. Finally, I'll also be attending statewide clerk conferences. All of this is in-line with the pastor's direction. For the progressive development of the church, as well as the community. We should all do our part to promote pastor's vision."

"Thank you, sister Macy. Anyone else?"

No one else had announcements. Therefore, Pastor McCoy ended bible study with a prayer then everyone went home.

Chapter Eleven

Disbelief

Saturday morning; which was the main event, the day people all over the United States prepared their bodies for the Jacksonville Ironman Triathlon; which was 72.3 miles which included jogging, bike riding, and swimming. It was 5:00 a.m. in the morning. Jerome and Joanne were going over their checklist before leaving home and making the 10-minute drive to the starting point. As the couple sat in the car in their driveway, Jerome made the first phone call.

"Good morning," Brother Calvin greeted as he answered his cell phone. Pastor, how do you feel today; are you ready?"

"Yes, I'm making my final calls. How are things with you, your checklist, and your team?"

"All is well; we're prepared. I need to make two more phone calls but everything looks good."

"That's good to hear. I'll see you at the starting point soon. Bye."

"Bye pastor."

Pastor Jerome ended his conversation with Calvin then made his second phone call.

"Hello," said Evelyn.

"Sister Evelyn, this is Pastor McCoy. I'm just going over my checklist. How are you and Jason?"

"We're well; we're in the parking lot trying to park now."

"Okay, you're early but that's good. Joanne and I will be there in a few minutes. Bye."

Disbelief

"Bye pastor."

Joanne was sitting in the driver's seat, driving her husband's car. She backed out of the driveway and commenced to the meeting spot which was a large, parking lot between San Marco Blvd. and Palm Ave. The Jacksonville Ironman Triathlon was to begin at 6:30 a.m. and all runners had to check-in before 6:00 a.m. The finish line was located at Metropolitan Park; the race would end at 11:30 p.m. It was estimated that 20% of the competitors would finish the race in roughly 10 hours–4:30 p.m., and 20% would not finish due to time constraints. The day's race would begin in a large, parking lot off of San Marco Blvd. The route would continue onto I-95 S to I-295 N to the Buckman Bridge. The swim portion would take place under the Buckman Bridge across the St. Johns River. Next, a bike ride from I-295 N to I-10 E back to I-95 S across I-295 N, and then back to the Buckman Bridge for another swim. Once out of the water, participants would jog to the I-295 N intersection, I-95 S. The next cycling segment would be south on I-295 S to Arlington Expy and Hart Bridge Expy; finishing with the final jog to the finish line.

Jerome and Joanne arrived at the parking lot and quickly noticed many members from the church. Most of whom were there to provide moral support for him and Jason. Sofia and Coleen were there as well, but not for the same reasons as most of the other congregants. In addition, many of Evelyn's friends and co-workers were in attendance. Pastor McCoy and his wife exited their vehicle and walked toward Evelyn's car to check on Jason. Many of Evelyn's friends were chatting amongst themselves when they saw the handsome looking Pastor McCoy, who Evelyn had told them about, walking in their direction.

"Evelyn, is that him?" Evelyn's co-worker, Helen, asked this in a low voice. However, four other ladies heard Helen. As a result, they stopped what they were doing and looked as well.

Helen was known to be a flirt, as well as an airhead and easy to get with. She was a size 14 and attractive; she was a fun-loving person who loved to enjoy herself and was always the life of the party. Unbeknown to her friends, she was a 38-year-old virgin. She was attractive to black men, but afraid to let her friends and family members know that, because of how she was raised in Portland Oregon, which was not to like black people.

"Yes, he and his wife," Evelyn replied with an emphasis on wife.

"Girl, I see why you never miss a Sunday in church. He's a hottie."

"Watch yourself. He is walking with his wife," Evelyn uttered in an undertone.

"Sister Evelyn, how are you again?" Pastor McCoy inquired as he gave Evelyn a hug and kiss.

"My name is Helen," Helen introduced herself as she extended her hand, flirting with Pastor McCoy. Before Pastor McCoy could reply to Helen's act of kindness, Joanne extended her hand and shook Helen's hand instead.

Joanne greeted, "Nice to meet you Helen. My name is Joanne Sharanay McCoy." The rest of Evelyn's friends, as well as Sofia and Coleen observed Joanne's actions. Thus, they remained quiet.

"Jason, today is the big day, buddy. Let's get started. The race begins in less than 30 minutes," Jerome said to Jason. Calvin and David showed up soon thereafter.

"Good morning Pastor and everyone else! How is everyone?" David greeted everyone in his flamboyant way.

Calvin approached everyone – Pastor McCoy, Joanne, Jason, Evelyn, and her friends and spoke to them. He said good morning to each individual and introduced himself to the people he didn't know.

"I'm great! Let's get Jason in the chair and in position," Jerome responded.

Calvin, David, and Pastor McCoy strapped Jason in his wheelchair for the first part of the race, which was a 19-mile jog. Sofia and Coleen stood next to the men as if they were assisting.

"Why so many cameras?" David asked Calvin.

"I don't know, ask the ones with the cameras," was Calvin's response.

David walked toward Evelyn's friends then inquired, "Why so many cameras, ladies?"

"Social media baby! This race has been talked about for the past four weeks, so we're recording the entire event and placing it on social media for the whole world to watch. Pastor McCoy and Jason are going to be famous," said Lisa, one of Evelyn's co-workers.

"What…wait a minute…you ladies are making a movie?"

"My name is Lisa. I'm one of Evelyn's co-workers. How may I help you?" Lisa inquired. Lisa was an attractive white female who was now flirting with David.

"My name is David; Evelyn and I attend the same church. So the whole race is going to be on social media?"

"Yes," Lisa replied with an exceptionally sexy smile.

"Can we finish this conversation later? I need to help my team get in position for the start of the race," David asked rhetorically and then walked toward Calvin and Pastor McCoy to provide assistant.

"I look forward to it," Lisa replied as she walked toward Evelyn. She had questions about David.

"Evelyn, who is the handsome man in the blue and white shorts next to the pastor?" One of Evelyn's friends, named Linda, inquired.

Linda was not as attractive as Evelyn or Helen. She was from West Virginia and was born and raised in the mountains. She married when she was young, at the age of thirteen and her husband was very abusive physically and mentally. After ten years of marriage and four-miscarriaged she got up the strength to run away and never returned home to visit. She did keep in touch with her mother and sisters by writing letters, but hated her father and brothers for not protecting her from her husband. She was short, 5'1" and slightly overweight, between a size 16 and 18. And has a desire to marry and adopt children.

"That's Kalevi. He's the pastor's armor bearer," Coleen answered.

"And he's homeless," Sofia added.

Joanne overheard the ladies talking, but ignored them and walked away.

"Social media, Lisa told me..." Calvin interrupted David.

"Lisa, bro! We're here to work not flirt. Think with your big head, not the little one."

"Calvin, listen to me. She, I mean Lisa, told me that on social media they've been talking about this race for weeks and we're going to be famous."

"We're not in the race; we're the helpers. Do you mean Pastor McCoy and Jason are going to be famous?"

"And us."

"Let's go," Calvin conveyed. David walked closer to the rest of the team.

Joanne led the group in prayer. As soon as she was done, Pastor McCoy wheeled Jason toward the starting point, turned around, looked at his wife and Kalevi and then told them, "Remember to bring the O2 and stretcher to the finish line. I'm leaving all I have on the track." Joanne had tears of joy in her eyes as she nodded her head. As Pastor McCoy and Jason waited in line to begin the race, he looked over and saw several church members there to support him and Jason. Surprisingly, he saw Carroll Benson approaching Evelyn. Jerome was focusing on the race. He had 19.5 miles until he would be swimming in the St. Johns Rivers. It was 6:30 a.m. and the runners were off.

Calvin, David, Joanne, and many others returned to the parking lot where they set up a makeshift command center. The first report came in.

"Calvin," is how he answered his cell phone.

"This is Mark. They're approaching me now, time 7:10," Mark announced, using his smartphone. Mark took a picture and uploaded it to social media outlets – *Facebook, Instagram,* and *Twitter.*

"Thank you," Calvin replied as he hung up and looked at Joanne. "The pastor may be running too fast; so far he's averaging seven minutes a mile while pushing a wheelchair."

The team relaxed in their chairs; Lisa and David were talking on the sideline and Carroll was trying to have a conversation with Evelyn. Joanne noticed Kalevi was about six cars down, talking to someone in a black, Jeep Cherokee. He appeared to be on a computer and the lady in the car looked like Lori. She moved around to get a better look at things.

****

Carroll's cell phone rang. "Excuse me," Carroll said to Evelyn as he reached for his phone and walked away. Evelyn walked to the area where Joanne and Calvin were sitting.

"Hello, how are you?"

"Carroll, this is Dwight. I completed my investigation and I'm ready to brief you and your friends. How is noon today?"

"Is the information good?"

"It's good to me. It's what you all paid for. Plus, it's information the Federal Government doesn't want you all to know about."

"Okay, I hope so."

"Noon it is." Dwight stated before disconnecting the call.

Then Carroll made a call to his sister. "Brenda, tell your church people to be at my place by noon today. The investigation is over and we're going to be updated at my place. I was told the information is good. See you there."

Brenda didn't answer, so Carroll left a message on her cell phone. Carroll looked at Evelyn with her friends and decided to leave. He waved goodbye and walked away.

****

Pastor McCoy and Jason were approaching a large crowd of supporters as they neared the Buckman Bridge on the Mandarin side. He was overwhelmed by the attention they were receiving. He was on the paved road of I-295 and continued as far as he could on the grass until he saw members of his team signal him to stop. A member of his team brought the inflatable boat and placed it in the water. Pastor McCoy stopped, removed his shirt, shoes, socks, and shorts. With only his swim trunks on, he reached into the jogger wheelchair, unstrapped Jason, picked him up, and proceeded to the boat in the river. Pastor McCoy strapped Jason in the boat, waded out a few yards where the water was waist-deep, and pulled a rope that was attached to the boat. Then he tied the loose end of the rope around his shoulder and waist and started swimming across the St. Johns River to the Orange Park side.

"Hello."

"This is Carl. They're in the water and swimming the St. Johns River, my time 9:48, on schedule."

"Thank you Carl," Calvin said as he hung up the phone.

Carl uploaded a short video of Pastor McCoy and Jason on the social media outlets. Lisa and David walked over to the area where Joanne, Calvin, and Evelyn were sitting and viewed the short video Carl uploaded with the pastor in his swim shorts, displaying his sexy body. Joanne smiled as she watched her sexy, handsome husband on video and the response of some of the ladies.

"Hey guys, we have videos and pictures all over the social media world. This is *Facebook*," David announced as he showed videos recorded by friends of Evelyn and Lisa.

"He is fine in those trunks," Helen said out loud as everyone watched the video that had been uploaded to *Facebook* and other outlets. Evelyn knew her friend, Helen, was a flirt. She also knew the first lady was not the type to remain quiet, so she took aggressive action.

"Helen, please walk with me to the restroom." Adhering to Evelyn's request, the two ladies walked away.

It was 10:50 a.m. Jason and Pastor McCoy had arrived in Orange Park. Pastor McCoy walked to land, pulling the inflatable boat along. He unstrapped Jason, removed his wet clothes, dressed him in a dry sweatsuit then placed him in the bicycle wheelchair. Pastor McCoy quickly ate two bananas and a sandwich. While eating his sandwich, he pulled his biker shorts over his swim trunks, quickly put on a pair of socks and shoes, a shirt with his number displayed on it, and continued the race.

"Is everything okay?" Joanne asked Calvin as she noticed him looking at his watch and cell phone.

"All is well. I was hoping we would have a status report by now," Calvin conveyed as his cell phone rang.

"This is Andy. They're out of the water and on the bike. My time is 11:12 a.m."

"Andy, how are things on your end?"

"All is well over here. Why do you ask?"

"My estimation is they should have departed your location five to seven minutes ago."

"I agree. He changed Jason's clothes and then ate a sandwich and two bananas."

"Okay, bye."

"Bye, until next time."

****

Chi Yang ran to his workstation after hearing the ringing noise from his computer. He recognized the sound well since he selected that particular tone to go off when there was a facial recognition match. Moreover, as a member of the Ministry of State of Security (MSS) he understood that it was an alert for a high priority case within the Chinese Intelligence Agency. Chi returned to his workstation and quickly reviewed the information displayed on his monitor. Promptly printing the data, he ran down the hall of The Embassy of the People's Republic of China in Washington, D.C. and entered the office of his supervisor, Kang Hsieh.

"Facial recognition sir," Chi said to Kang as he interrupted Kang's phone conversation.

"Who?" Kang asked this with the phone still to his face.

"Robert Sammy Johnson, 75% match." Kang disconnected the phone without alerting the person on the other end. Recognizing the name, he realized it was a high priority case and had been for more than thirty years.

Hastily examining the printout Kang received from Chi, Kang picked up the secured phone on his desk and began dialing a number for Beijing. "He looks young," Kang said to Chi.

"The Americans are good at staying off the grid," Chi replied.

****

Disbelief

While the Ironman race was in progress, Carroll was holding a special meeting at his home. He was hoping the information Dwight had was enough to get rid of Pastor McCoy. Although Carroll knew that people were really taking a liking to the pastor, and voting him out of office was impossible, he was hoping there was something in his background that would force him to resign. Carroll believed Pastor McCoy was a threat to him ever having a relationship with Evelyn. Even though Carroll had only met Pastor McCoy once and never saw Joanne, he was familiar with the rumors about her. Carroll believed Pastor McCoy was an everyday, nice-looking, well-educated, white male who married an attractive, quick-thinking, fast-talking, black female with hustling skills. Evelyn was the exact female who could make the pastor leave his attractive, street-smart, black wife for. However, Carroll was determined to have Evelyn for himself.

There were about ten men in Carroll's home waiting to hear what Dwight had to say: Willie Long, Chairman of the Deacons; Lawrence Clock, Assistant Chairman of the Deacons; Kenneth Loupe, Deacon and Trustee; James McDonald, Chairman of the Trustees; Joseph Hopes, Trustee; George Logan, City Manager and Trustee; Robert Brunel, Mayor; Danny Salesman, Lieutenant with the Jacksonville Police Department; as well as Tyrone Cumming, President of the ushers. Although Robert and Danny told everyone they were out, Carroll refused to accept their resignations.

"Gentlemen, I'm so glad you were all able to make it on such short notice. I hope the information you learn here today is rewarding to you all. After all, this is what you paid for. Any questions before I get started?"

"Did you need more than the initial $10,000?" James asked.

"You paid $45,000 for the information you're getting today. In all honesty, it's worth much more and I'm sure you'll all agree once you've heard it. I may write a book about it when it's all over," Dwight said with a smile and chuckle.

"Who paid the additional $35,000?" Willie asked.

"Carroll is my point of contact, so ask him about the details," was Dwight's reply.

"I can give everyone the breakdown later. Let's hear the report now," Carroll announced, knowing he paid the entire $45,000.

"The person you know as Pastor Doctor Jerome Samiah McCoy from Rainer Beach, Seattle, Washington, whose parents are Jerome and Pauline McCoy, is not true." Everyone in the room started hitting each other with high fives. Carroll had a huge smile on his face. "Please let me finish before the celebration." Everyone returned to their seats.

"Pastor McCoy was born Jerold Sammy Johnson to Robert and Ruby Johnson in Arlington, Virginia. His mother was a history teacher at Langley High School and his father was employed by The Central Intelligence Agency. Yes, the CIA, as a spy working in Central Africa. He had one sister, Shelly, and one brother, Robert, Jr."

"His father's friend and co-worker, Richard Turner, married his high school love Pearl McCoy, a Human Resource Analyst at the Pentagon. The couple had three children, two girls, Samantha and Faith, and one son, Jonathan."

"Put your seatbelts on boys. Somewhere around June 1975, Richard Turner, a black male working with Robert Johnson, a white male, was assigned to the Central African Republic region to prevent the spread of the Chinese government influences in that district. In August of 1980, both ladies, Ruby Johnson and Pearl Turner, along with their children, boarded a plane that departed from Dulles International Airport to Johannesburg, South Africa for a 17-day vacation. Both families were heading out to meet their husbands and dads. On August 21, 1980, the local media reported that local thugs robbed, raped, and killed two American families living in the Protea Hotel Parktonian. The U.S. Government accepted that as the official cause of their death. Now, here's the twist. Neither Richard Turner's body nor the body of Jerold Sammy Johnson, who was only one day shy of his first birthday, was ever found."

"It was assumed that Richard made it back to the U.S. and settled in South Seattle where he raised Jerold. He adopted his wife's maiden name McCoy and gave the young boy the name of Jerome Samiah McCoy."

"Question. Did the CIA ever get revenge for what happened to the two families?" Willie asked.

"I have nothing official on that, but one year later, on August 21, 1981, eight Chinese embassies were bombed. Over the next eight years, on August 21, eight different embassies were bombed each year. The official word was that a small, unorganized, terrorist group was responsible for the bombings. The rumor was that a rogue agent was seeking retaliation," Dwight answered.

Willie spoke up with a question. "How do you people, the intelligence community, determine the difference between a terrorist and non-terrorist group?"

"Well, most of the time a terrorist group is seeking attention. They leave a message such as a name or symbol or post something to social media accepting credit. Unlike the U.S. government, the Chinese and many other governments shoot first then ask questions. We want proof and facts before retaliating. China doesn't operate that way, so the chance of a terrorist group attacking a place like China is small. Since they've been attacked by their own weapons, it indicates that a rogue agent is using China's weapons, missiles, and explosives to attack Chinese embassies."

"I'm so confused," Willie said.

"Well, that is the pastor. The man who raised him is his father's, friend, and co-worker. He played sports in middle and high school, graduated from Lake High School and earned his BA and Master degree from the University of Washington. He grew up in the local church where his father, Richard

Turner, I mean Jerome McCoy, served as a Deacon and is an active member today."

"Question, do you think his father, the man who raised him, still has contacts at the agency? Do you think he knows you have this information?" Willie asked.

"I never thought about that. It has been thirty years plus. I feel safe in saying no. On the other hand, I have no way of really knowing," Dwight responded.

"I would hate for us to get shot for knowing this information. I've seen some TV shows that I know the information is factual and based on actual places," Willie replied.

"Pastor McCoy and Joanne grew up as neighbors. They went to their high school prom as a couple. Now for Joanne…"

"Question, does Pastor McCoy know what happened to his parents, brother, and sister?" Willie asked.

Dwight was tired of Willie's questions. He wanted to share his findings with everyone but Willie was engrossed with life as a spy. "Men, please allow me to provide you with all the information. We've been here for more than an hour now and I still have so much more to reveal."

"I agree," Carroll added.

"Now Joanne, she's not as complicated as her husband. She was born Joanne Sharanay McKinney in South Seattle, Washington; she grew up as a neighbor, next door to be exact, to Jerome Samiah McCoy. Both of them attended the same elementary, middle, and high school, as well as the same church and college, University of Washington. Joanne graduated from high school in June. That same month, she was enrolled as a student at Gary Manual Aveda Institute. By the age of 21, she owned her first salon; it was a birthday gift from her boyfriend, who is now her husband. Him and his father remodeled a neighborhood corner store into a hair salon. JOSAM is the name of her chain of high-end hair salons. Within the next twelve years, she completed her BA in Psychology and MA degree in Hospitality Business Management from the University of Washington, and extended her salons throughout Washington, Oregon, and Northern California. Owning 28 in total and currently working as a business consultant for hotels, restaurants, and other businesses in the Southern Georgia and Northern Florida areas. She's worth millions of dollars, maybe as much as fifty million or more."

Everyone in the room was shocked as they listened to the report on Joanne.

"Excuse me, that information is not remotely close to what we received from the previous investigation report," James stated abruptly.

"I understand and the reason is there was a misspelled name. There is a Joanne McKinney who's the person I just told you about and your first lady. Then there is a Joanne McKinnis, whose profile you all received from your investigator. Joanne McKinnis is the one who served time and her education is limited to Cosmetology school. Furthermore, Joanne McKinnis works for your first lady. She manages one of her salons and they all went to the same school."

***

"Boss, we followed Dwight to a home in Jacksonville, Florida that's owned by a Carroll Benson, a reformed thug. It appears he's having a meeting with people from the church Jerome is pastoring," Wendy Catchin said to her supervisor, Neo Bullright, who was located at a CIA substation in Miami, Florida.

"Watch them," Neo responded as he hung up the phone with Wendy then received a call from Quenton Barnwell, who was stationed at a CIA substation in Manhattan, New York.

"Yes," Neo greeted Quenton as he answered the phone.

"Robert Sammy Johnson, the name is floating on the Chinese network, will report back when I learn more." Quenton summarized then disconnected the call.

Neo spoke to himself "After thirty plus years of rest, things are about to heat up."

Neo was a retired Green Beret that is contracted by the CIA; his job was to protect retired CIA officials and their families, as well as active agency as determined by the nature of their work. Neo is ten years younger than Richard and his nephew. Richard's wife and Neo's mother were sisters. Neo had been keeping Richard off the Chinese's radar for the past twelve years. However, now with social media and face recognition software it was possible they would find him.

****

"He's averaging 6½ minutes per mile on the bike; which is extremely good. Out of all the people competing today, he's still in the top 20%." Calvin announced this to everyone at the makeshift operation center that was moved from the parking lot to Metropolitan Park.

Sofia and Coleen were still acting as if they didn't know one another. Kalevi had not arrived to the current location; everyone thought he was still with the lady in the black Jeep.

"Well I have the O2 and stretcher ready as he directed," Joanne declared.

"How many people are in the race today?" Helen inquired.

"Approximately 7,500," David yelled out as he continued to flirt with Lisa.

"Who's preaching tomorrow?" Calvin asked.

"A guest preacher," Joanne replied.

"First Lady, I really enjoy you and Pastor's teaching style. Any recommendations for me?" Calvin asked.

"Study and pray, pray and study."

Disbelief

****

"Willie, why do you keep looking out the window?" Carroll asked.

"Truthfully, this information really scares me. The CIA, the Chinese, and assassin hit teams make me think something is terribly wrong. As far as we know, all of that research could have triggered some type of red flag, an alert or something. They could have followed him and be listening to our conversation," Willie admitted as he pointed at Dwight. "He could have led them to us."

"I'm assuming this is something you've seen on TV or the movies," Carroll expressed.

"And if I did, so what? How do we know the movies aren't based on true events, and the government hasn't been denying it for years? After all the proof that Area 51 really does exist in the desert, the government still denies it. Why is that?"

"You are one paranoid black man. Do you see any black SUVs outside?" Carroll asked.

"Why do you ask that?" Willie countered as he continued to peer into the streets.

"Because Government agencies drive black SUVs," Dwight retorted.

"No..."

"Yes," Dwight replied and then continued, "At the end of the block, around the corner, there is a black SUV. I can only see the hood, but trust me, it's a large SUV." Everyone in the room started looking at each other and out the windows. Due to the fear resonating among the men, the room got quiet. "Gentlemen, I'm leaving this place. If that SUV drives off after me, don't contact me again. If it doesn't, protect yourselves," Dwight voiced as he packed up all of his equipment and started walking out of Carroll's home. Carroll stopped him at the door.

"Dwight, we have the mayor and the police department here. Let us help you."

"If I triggered something, this thing will be way out of your league. During my investigation, Richard Turner and Robert Johnson have additional family members in that line of work. Stay here and relax. I'll be fine; I haven't committed a crime," Dwight advised as he opened the door, went outside, got into his vehicle, and drove off.

****

Ming-hug Yu, Director of the MSS, was awakened by the ringing sound of his secured phone, which was located on his nightstand in the bedroom of his home. Comprehending it was part of the job to be awakened at midnight, and since it was his secured line, he understood it was important. "Yes," Ming-hug answered.

"Facial recognition, Robert Sammy Johnson," Kang Hsieh said. At the mention of Robert Johnson's name, Ming-hug sat up in his bed.

"Dispatch an information gathering team to his location, then collect everything you have and call me in eight hours at the office." Ming-hug instructed as he hung up the phone and returned to his slumber.

****

"They're approaching the end of the 26 mile run; it's almost over now. There's only the bike ride and one mile jog left. They're in the top 40%." Calvin reported this as he talked to friends on the cell phone.

"Look at social media. People all over the world are commenting on Jason and Pastor McCoy," David conveyed.

"Joanne, I'm really surprised pastor was ready on such short notice for the race; and why are they here?" Evelyn stated as she directed her attention at Sofia and Coleen.

"What you guys don't know about the pastor is he's wanted to compete in this type of race for a long time. For years, he's been training his body for cycling, swimming, and running. Unfortunately, he always had an excuse not to compete. A few times, he went as far as to sign up, but never showed up on the day of the competition. Conversely, when Brother David talked to him about Jason, he felt the Lord had been preparing him for this day, not for himself, but for Jason. As a result, it didn't require much preparation for him to get in physical shape. All that was needed was mental conditioning to ready himself for the race." Joanne ignored the question about Sofia and Coleen; the two women sat off from everyone else as if they were better or outsiders.

****

"Your friend, Dwight, has been gone for a few hours. The SUV is gone as well. I'm out of here," said Lieutenant Danny Salesman, as others in the room stood, and prepared to leave Carroll Benson's home as well.

"Men, what do we do with this information?" Carroll asked.

"Forget it; forget it all, if you have any common sense," Danny answered as he continued to his car with many others following him.

****

"Pastor and Jason should be coming down the road very soon," said Calvin as they all waited close to the finish line with the local media recording each racer. They were especially waiting on the local church pastor, who was competing with a handicapped child.

"I see them coming!" David yelled.

Joanne looked out and saw her husband running the last mile of the race. She recognized he was running fast and giving it all he had. The crowd was going crazy. The pastor was helping the handicapped, which was commendable.

Joanne quickly remembered what her husband told her–'Have the oxygen and stretcher ready at the finish line; I'm leaving it all on the track.' "The air!" Joanne gasped as she grabbed the portable oxygen. "Get the stretcher," she yelled out to Calvin and Kalevi then started running closer to the finish line to meet her husband. Evelyn and her friends took off running behind Joanne. Calvin grabbed the portable stretcher, and then Kalevi and David proceeded to jog to the finish line as well.

Pastor McCoy crossed the finish line, slowly going from jogging to walking. His skin was pale and he was unaware of his surroundings. When he released the runner's wheelchair that Jason was resting in, the wheelchair went in one direction and Pastor McCoy slowly walked in another. Kalevi was in front of Joanne and very close to the pastor. Joanne shouted, "Get Jason!" She pointed toward the wheelchair, but continued to head toward her husband. Kalevi redirected his path toward the pastor and went in the direction of Jason's wheelchair.

Jerome saw Joanne and stopped walking and smiled. Just as Joanne reached Jerome, he collapsed into her arms and they slowly descended to the ground, holding onto each other. Joanne quickly placed the portable oxygen mask on Jerome's face. Evelyn went to her son, Jason, taking control of the chair from Kalevi. "Go help Joanne," Evelyn directed Kalevi, who went to aid Joanne with the pastor. Slowly repositioning the wheelchair, Evelyn pushed it toward Joanne and Jerome. Calvin, David, and two other men arrived on the scene. They saw Joanne on the grass holding her husband with an air mask on his face. Confused as to what to do or say, everyone stared at Joanne as she embraced the pastor.

"Is he okay?" Evelyn asked.

"I'm sure he will be. Let's get him on the stretcher and out of here," Joanne requested.

Calvin, David, and other volunteers opened the portable stretcher, placing it beneath Pastor McCoy as Joanne kept the mask over his nose and moved him to a tent.

159

Disbelief

After approximately 15 minutes of rest, the pastor was strong enough to walk to his car and go home. People, most of whom were representatives of the media, surrounded him. Members of the church accompanied the Pastor McCoy and Joanne to their car. Joanne opened the trunk of the car, removing a large box full of large manila envelopes, and then handed the box to Calvin.

"Calvin, please distribute these to each person and let me know if I've forgotten anyone."

"Will do First Lady." Each envelope was a thank you package from the pastor and first lady, containing season tickets to the Jacksonville Jaguars' games, a $100 gift certificate for the Jacksonville Landing, a four-night stay at any Hilton hotel, and tickets for their entire family to Disney World and Universal Studios.

Each individual gradually departed the park and commenced their road trip home. Sofia and Coleen arrived at the vacant location and noticed their cars were gone. They called the Jacksonville Police Department and reported their vehicles as being stolen or towed. The operator dispatched a local police officer to their location. Upon the officer's arrival, he exited his squad car and approached Sofia and Coleen.

"Ms. Sofia Gomez and Coleen Walker, I'm assuming," the police officer stated.

"Yes." Both women replied.

"So a Jaguar is what you, Ms. Sofia drive; and Ms. Coleen, you drive a Mercedes Benz. Is that correct?"

"Yes!" They replied again, more angry than the first time.

"Ladies, no cars have been towed from this location today. Do either of you have ID?"

"Sir, look at the way we're dressed; we only have our cell phones with us." Coleen spoke up, referring to the skimpy, tight, sexy shorts and t-shirts they were attired in.

"Well more sad news, we ran your names with the DMV database and there aren't vehicles registered in either of your names. Even more interesting, is neither of you have a driver's license."

"What! Sofia yelled.

"Is there someone you ladies can call?" the officer asked politely.

Coleen and Sofia went to use their cell phones and they both were dead.

"You Bitch!" Coleen shouted, referring to Joanne McCoy.

"Sir, can you give us a ride home? We live in the Beau Rivage Condos."

The police officer doubted what Sofia and Coleen were telling him, but was willing to go the extra mile. The women got in the back seat of the patrol car and the officer drove them to the condo community. Coleen typed in her pin to open the access-controlled gate but the pin didn't work.

"My pin isn't working." The police glared at the women as if they were actually lying to him about their car being stolen, as well as them living in the Beau Rivage community.

"Let me try my pin." Sofia stated; they all quickly realized her pin didn't work either.

"Ladies, we need to leave this place," the officer informed them.

"No, we live here." Both Sofia and Coleen replied.

"Let's call security," Coleen suggested, as she picked up the phone next to the gate and dialed the security guard on duty.

"Hello, this is Mr. Bentley. How may I help you?"

"My name is Coleen Walker. I live on the west wing, unit C-7001; my pin is not working, can you let me in please?"

"Not a problem; just let me verify you in the system." Coleen turned around and looked at the policeman with an expression that said, I told you we live here.

"Ms. Coleen, you spell your name C-o-l-e-e-n?" Mr. Bentley asked.

"Yes." Coleen replied.

"There is no Coleen Walker in the system, which means no Coleen lives here."

"What! Check again; I live here!" Coleen exclaimed heatedly.

"Ma'am, I checked a few times. I also looked at the printed copy. Coleen Walker does not reside here."

"What about you ma'am?" the officer asked Sofia.

"Really there's no use; no use at all," Sofia responded.

"Can I give you ladies a ride?" the policeman asked.

"No," replied Sofia.

"Yes," replied Coleen.

"To where?" Sofia asked.

"Who else? Demetrius!"

Sofia and Coleen entered the backseat of the police cruiser for a courtesy ride across town to Demetrius's home. Twenty minutes later, they arrived at his residence, which was in the Chimney Lakes community on the West Side of Jacksonville. The officer was way out of his jurisdiction and risked being reprimanded if his supervisor discovered it. Sofia and Coleen exited the vehicle and walked to Demetrius's front door and then the policeman quickly drove off.

"Coming!" Demetrius shouted as he responded to the sound of his doorbell. "Ladies, this is a surprise; a big surprise after our last meeting at the Ritz Carlton.

"Your girlfriend decided to bite back," Coleen informed him as she and Sofia entered his living room.

"Please come in and make yourselves at home," Demetrius expressed with a little sarcasm in his voice.

"D, our cars have been stolen, cell phones turned off, and we're locked out of our condo. Plus, the police officer told us we're not registered with the DMV and don't have driver's licenses. Who could do this; who would do this?"

"Ladies, you two have made a lot of enemies in the last six to eight years. I told you to leave the area about two years ago, but you didn't take my advice. Instead, you chose to do two more good years of additional hustling while making more enemies. What do you want from me?"

"Who is doing this to us?"

"I have no clue; but you can start with all those people you hustled. How many families have you separated; how many children's college funds have you pilfered; how many wives and husbands have you embarrassed? Think about all the CEOs, government officials, and wives you've defrauded. You've both made a lot of enemies."

"I think it's Joanne," Coleen alleged.

"No, she's computer illiterate."

"Maybe she hired someone?" Sofia guessed.

"That's possible, but I have no clue."

"We need a place to sleep."

"You guys aren't staying here!"

"D..." Coleen started.

"No!"

"Why not?" asked Sofia.

Disbelief

Demetrius walked over to a closet in the room, reached into his coat pocket, removed $800 in cash and then went back to Sofia and Coleen.

"Foremost, I have a date tonight. Second, I can't afford the attention you ladies receive or would bring to my home and or business. Here's all the cash I have; take it and go. That's all I can do for you."

"Can we use one of your cars?" Coleen asked.

"No!"

"D, who is doing this to us!?"

"Look, both of you antagonized a multitude of individuals. I suggest you get to the banks early Monday morning."

"We have no ID," Sofia replied.

"Damn, goodbye ladies and good luck." Sofia and Coleen left Demetrius's home with $400 each in cash and two cell phones with no service.

Chapter Twelve

Pastor's Love

"**B**abe will you please answer the phone! It's been ringing all morning. Who in the heck keeps calling?" Jerome asked Joanne this as he relaxed in the large La-Z-Boy chair in their bedroom wearing his black satin robe with a cup of coffee in his hand. He was reminiscing over the previous day's event – the Ironman race.

"It's the church babe. They want you to come to church as soon as possible. I've been telling them that you need your rest, but they keep calling and I'm really getting upset over it."

"What's going on?" Jerome asked just prior to one of three of his cell phones ringing. They were used for church business, which is not the number he gave to all members of the church. Joanne picked up her husband's smart phone from the nightstand in the bedroom and looked at the caller ID. She handed Jerome his Samsung S5 and said, "It's Calvin, your partner." Jerome took the cell phone from his wife.

"Thank you, pretty woman." Jerome said to his wife. "Hello, this is Pastor McCoy how can I help you?" Jerome listened to Calvin talk for 30 seconds then hung up. He turned to Joanne and said, "We're going to the church. How soon before you're ready to leave?"

"What was said on the phone?"

"I'll tell you while we're driving to the church. Get dressed please," Jerome said as he got up and walked into the huge bathroom within their bedroom and enjoyed a nice, but quick morning shower. Jerome noticed Joanne combing her hair in the mirror. Jerome knew Joanne usually did her hair last, just prior to putting on her shoes. Her routine consisted of taking a shower, oiling down her nude body, slipping into her undergarments, meticulously preparing her makeup, and adorning her body with jeweled accessories. It wasn't until then that she considered herself fully dressed for an event.

However, he was rushing against time and she was doing her hair first. He was angry but maintained his cool as she stood in the large mirror in their bathroom. Jerome exited the shower and noticed his wife was still in the mirror, wearing her sky-blue silk bathrobe. "Babe, First Lady, we need to move with the quickness. Please get dressed," Jerome asked as he dried his body and put on his undershorts and undershirt. Joanne calmly walked into the walk-in closet inside the master bedroom and came out with red and black, three-inch heel dress shoes. Jerome angrily entered the same closet and came out with a tan suit and yellow dress shirt. He was looking at his wife, who was still wearing her bathrobe. Joanne placed her shoes on her feet then removed her robe; she was dressed in a fitted red and black dress.

"Babe, I'm ready and waiting on you," Joanne said as she smiled at Jerome who looked surprised as he gazed at his beautiful and attractive wife while putting on his dress pants and shirt.

"How did you know?"

"We wives, we First Ladies, we just know these things. The Lord Jesus has gifted us with First Lady virtues."

"First Lady virtues."

"I know you've never heard of it, but it's real. I want to know about the phone call between you and Calvin."

Jerome and his wife exited their house, got into their car and then proceeded to drive to Abundant Truth Baptist Church.

"About a month ago, Calvin explained to me why so many people in the church were giving me such a hard time. It's both slightly funny and sad, but it is what it is."

"And why is that?"

"The people wanted to hire an African-American pastor. When they viewed my CDs, they weren't able to see the video they could only hear the audio portion. They loved the preaching and teaching, so they hired me. Once they realized I wasn't a black male, which was the day we arrived in Jacksonville, they wanted me to quit. They would have been successful if you had allowed me to."

"But today?"

"Calvin earned status; he was able to accomplish what others failed to do. He will be a great Deacon or Youth Pastor, as well as a Trustee and member of any board I can get him on."

"Sounds like you're making long term plans – strategizing."

"I am a true believer in praying and fasting, so I know the Lord Jesus will work everything out as we serve and love Him. Also, I think it's smart to get like-minded people in the church in key positions. Calvin and I and a few others are like-minded; I need to get them in key positions. However, I can only plant the seed; our Lord Jesus will bring it to pass."

Jerome and his wife parked their vehicle in the church parking lot and were amazed at the number of cars parked around the church. They exited their car and walked into the church from a side door near the back of the building. They were listening to the ending of the 8:00 a.m. service. The guest preacher, Stacy Blackburn, from a local church, was scheduled to preach at the 8:00 a.m. and noon service so that Pastor McCoy could rest from the previous day's race. As Reverend Blackburn prepared to close out the 8:00 a.m. service, he looked out the window of the door next to the pulpit and spotted Pastor McCoy in the hallway and signaled with his hand for Pastor McCoy to come into the main sanctuary.

"Abundant Truth, your pastor, Pastor Jerome McCoy," Reverend Blackburn stretched out his hand toward the closed door as if he would magically appear on stage. Pastor McCoy walked in with his wife. Everyone in the church stood to their feet and started clapping their hands. The pastor and his wife walked in surprised to see the sanctuary full. Every inch of the church's pews was occupied as well as some chairs in the aisles. The two of them walked to the second step of the four-step staircase to the pulpit. They stopped and gave each other a very big, deep, and passionate kiss. Afterwards, Joanne turned around and stood next to the door they had just entered through, while Pastor McCoy walked to the pulpit and podium.

"Good morning Abundant Truth Baptist Church and guests!" Pastor McCoy yelled out to the congregation. There wasn't an empty seat in the church. This was a first in more than thirty years. "I'm not going to hold you long, but I'm glad you all came out and hope to see you all very soon. Reverend Blackburn, please close us out."

Reverenced Blackburn closed out the service and then he and the pastor returned to the pastor's office. Joanne went to her office and relaxed.

"Brother Tyrone, if noon service is anything like the 8:00 a.m. service, the church will be twice as full. You may need to ask additional ushers to be on duty today and we'll use the dining area as the overflow room," Willie said to Tyrone, as he prepared the church for the overflow, knowing more people came out to 11:30 a.m. service than the 8:00 a.m. service.

"I'm all over it, Chairman," Tyrone replied as he went to prepare for the noon rush.

"James, I think we should get the dining area ready for the overflow, and chairs in the aisles in the sanctuary. I'm expecting the church to be filled beyond capacity. We may have to turn some people away today."

"I was thinking the same thing; I'm on it now. Please let Beverly know," James replied.

"Quincy and Aaron, I'm in need of your help today as well as the help of your wives. Can you meet me out front by 11:00 a.m.? I'm making some changes in preparation of the noon crowd," Willie stated.

"Yes." Deacon Chair, Quincy, and Aaron replied in unison. Then James walked away.

"Brother Calvin and David, your service is needed today, please follow me." Willie quickly commanded them as he continued walking and talking.

"Yes Chairman," both men replied as they walked with Willie.

"I'm expecting a lot of people at the noon service. I want one of you assigned to the pastor's office and one assigned to the first lady's office. Stay with them, you two are security today; so keep people off them. Can you two do that for me? Please work with Kalevi."

Abundant Truth Baptist Church was designed to hold approximately 300 people in its sanctuary. It was estimated that 375 people attended the 8:00 a.m. service. The noon service was approaching. It was approximated that between the sanctuary, with chairs in the aisle, and the dining area, there would be more than 500 individuals attending the noon service. Pastor McCoy was in his office conversing with the guest speaker, Reverend Blackburn, when Joanne walked in. Calvin and David were outside the pastor's office, controlling traffic.

"Jerome, the people are here today to hear from you, not me. I think you should deliver the message today."

"My mind and body are not ready," Pastor McCoy responded.

"I understand, truly I do."

"Gentlemen, it's 12:15; the noon service started 45 minutes ago. One or both of you need to get in the pulpit because it's time to walk out now," Joanne stated firmly.

Reverend Blackburn looked at Pastor McCoy, realizing they couldn't enter the pulpit without a plan. Pastor McCoy looked at his wife, stood up from the chair behind his office desk, and proceeded out of his office and into the sanctuary. Reverend Blackburn was confused, but he followed as well. The two men walked out of the pastor's office, through the side door, and into the pulpit. Joanne took a seat on the center bench.

The praise and worship team took their seats. One of the Deacons prayed then turned the service over to the pulpit. Pastor McCoy took the podium as if he was preparing to preach.

"It's praying time church, so prepare your hearts and minds."

Pastor McCoy gazed out into the sanctuary and rested his eyes on the beautiful, sexy, first lady.

"First Lady, please come forward and lead us in prayer."

Joanne stood and walked to the podium that was off to the side of the pulpit, for use by those who are not pastors or ministers. She tested the microphone by saying, "Amen, Amen, Amen," in her normal tone of voice. When she recognized the microphone was working, she shouted in a louder voice, "Good morning saints! Does anyone here have something to thank Jesus for this morning? If you do, please give our Lord in Heaven some praise!" Everyone began clapping their hands and shouting various words of gratitude to the King Jesus. "If the Lord has been good to you all week and you're happy to be here, tell your neighbor that the Lord Jesus is good! If the blood in your body is still running warm and you have use of both hands and feet, you can see, smell, touch and taste, stand on your feet and give the Lord Jesus some praises!" Everyone in the church was out of their seat, shouting praises to the Lord Jesus.

Each individual in the church was talking to someone about how good the Lord Jesus had been to them. "Give someone a high five if the Lord Jesus has been good to you! Don't allow Satan to steal your chance to give back to Jesus what He has given you." Everyone was out of their seats, talking and slapping each other high fives. "Don't fool yourself and think the alarm clock woke you up or your wife or husband, or that you raised yourself out of your bed on your own strength, or the nerves and muscles in your body submitted to the order of your voice. You better know there's a God who decided you would wake up today, you would walk today, you would be here today, and today is not the day you will meet your maker or gather with your ancestors. Today, the Lord Jesus decided you would not depart Mother Earth." Everyone in the church was out of their seats and praising the Lord in their special way. Everyone was feeling the spirit of the Lord. The guest speaker was amazed at how Joanne energized and motivated the crowd. He was shocked as he became aware that the spirit of the Lord was upon her.

Reverend Blackburn was thinking to himself. "What is she doing, preaching, praying or having a special praise and worship moment?" He looked at Pastor McCoy, who was sitting next to him in the pulpit and unable to read how he felt. However, he did recognize that Pastor McCoy was peaceful as if he wasn't worried about what was taking place. He was confused, yet confident that the Pastor and First Lady had a special way of communicating.

"It's praying time saints. It's praying time…My Lord, my God, who can do anything but fail. We give thanks for this day. We thank you for this fragile world we live in, it's times and tides, it's sunsets and seasons, we give thanks this day. For the joy of human life, it's wonders and surprises, its hopes and achievements. We give thanks this day for our human community, our common past and future hopes, our oneness transcending all separation, our capacity to work for peace and justice in the midst of hostility and oppression. We give thanks this day for high hopes and noble causes, for faith without fanaticism, for understanding of views not shared. We give thanks this day for all who have labored and suffered for a fairer and peaceful world, who have lived so that others might live in dignity and freedom. We give thanks this day for human liberty and sacred rites, for opportunities to change and grow, to affirm and choose. We give thanks this day. We pray that we may live not by our fears, but by our hopes, not by our words, but by our deeds. Unto Him who is able to keep you from falling, and to present you faultless before the presence of his glory with exceeding joy, to the one and only wise God our Savior, be the glory and majesty, dominion and power, both now and forever. Amen."

Joanne turned around and gazed at her pastor, who smiled at her. Then she turned around and looked at the Minister of Music, Karen Lightfoot. The church was full of people. Regrettably, the pastor was too tired to preach and the guest preacher didn't feel adequate. She realized her next action was a bold move. Nonetheless, something had to be done and quickly. Therefore, she removed the microphone from the podium and began to walk down one of the aisles in the church.

"Just clap your hands like this…this is an old school jam. You know that He's good and His mercy endureth forever. Now we serve notice to depression, confusion, all manner of evil, and every sickness. No matter what comes next, I'm gonna stand up.

This is the day, this is the day

That the Lord has made, that the Lord has made

I will rejoice, I will rejoice

And be glad in it, and be glad in it

This is the day that the Lord has made

The First Lady

I will rejoice and be glad in it

This is the day, this is the day

That the Lord hath made"

The Minister of Music, Karen Lightfoot, directed the choir and musician to support Joanne via song and music. Joanne went on for the next three minutes and sang the old school song by Fred Hammond, "This Is The Day." As soon as she finished singing the song, Joanne began another song without delay.

"Did anyone come here today to praise the Lord? If you came here to praise our Lord in heaven Jesus Christ, please sing along with me.

Praise is what I do

When I want to be close to You,

I lift my hands in praise.

Praise is who I am,

I will praise Him while I can.

I'll bless Him at all times.

And I vow to praise You

Through the good and the bad.

I'll praise You,

Whether happy or sad.

I'll praise You

This is my testimony in all that I go through,

Because praise is what I do,

Cause I owe it all to You.

(Come on church)"

Everyone in the church was enjoying Joanne's singing. In addition to the choir and musician, they all sang along with her.

"Praise is what I do

(Come on church)

When I want to be close to You,

(I lift my hands–somebody lift Him)

I lift my hands in praise.

(Somebody say it so the devil will hear you)

Praise is who I am,

Come on praise the Lord"

Joanne and the church continued singing until they finished the song "Praise Is What I Do." Without pause, she started another song.

"Now that's a black woman who has her man's back," Richard said to his wife, Charlene Monk.

She has class, and she's very supportive of her husband, Charlene said to herself. Her pride wouldn't allow her to speak aloud anything positive about the first lady or agree with her husband.

"Be-e-e-e-e Grateful

Be-e-e-e-e Grateful

God has not promised me sunshine

That's not the way it's going to be

But a little rain (A little rain)

Mixed with God's sunshine

A little pain (A little pain)

Makes me appreciate the good times"

People who loved and knew the song, "Be Grateful" by Walter Hawkins, jumped to their feet and applauded for the song and its meaning.

"Pastor is not preaching today," Brenda said to her husband, Tyrone.

"Why do you say that?"

"All of these songs the first lady is singing. She's killing time, in place of preaching."

"She's just preparing the people for the word."

"Okay, time will tell, Mr. Man."

"Be-e-e-e-e-e Grateful

Be-e-e-e-e-e Grateful

God desires to feel your longings

Every pain that you feel

He feels them just like you (Just like you)

But he can't afford to let you feel only good (Only good)

Then you can't appreciate the good times"

Evelyn got out of her seat and walked to the kitchen area. She noticed the first lady had been singing and worshipping for the past 15 to 20 minutes. She went to the refrigerator, removed three bottles of water and then returned to the sanctuary. She listened as Joanne finished the Walter Hawkins song, "Be Grateful."

"My God said he'd never, never foresake you!

Be Grateful oh yeah!

God said he would, he would never, never forsake you!

Be Grateful oh yeah!

Be Grateful Hallelujah!

Oh! Be Grateful

Pastor's Love

The Lord is the light!"

Just as Joanne finished singing, Evelyn went over, handed her a bottle of water, took the microphone out of her hand, and turned around to face the congregation. Everyone was surprised to see Evelyn with the microphone as if she was going to sing.

"I just wanna make it to heaven"

Karen Lightfoot led the choir and the musician to follow Evelyn in the song. The church erupted in applause. Evelyn's praising voice was as pretty as she was as she started off with the song, "Well Done" by Deitrick Haddon. Joanne was off to the side resting, listening, enjoying, and drinking her water.

"I just wanna make it in

I just wanna cross that river

I wanna be free from sin

Oo, I just want my name written (Oh Lord)

Written in the Lamb's book of life

When this life is over

I just wanna have eternal life

Oh, I wanna hear Him say

Well done, well done, well done

You can come on in.

Anybody wanna hear Him say

Wave your hands where I can see 'em...

Anybody wanna see your loved ones

That you've lost along the way

I just wanna walk those streets of gold, yeah

They say the half have never, never been told

I don't want my singing Lord

176

The First Lady

I don't want it, to be in vain"

As Evelyn came to the conclusion of the song, "Well Done," Joanne walked toward Evelyn to take the microphone. To everyone's surprise, Evelyn turned away from Joanne and began to sing another song.

"For so long I was silent.

For so long I did not have a song of praise.

Depression filled my days and clouds blocked my ways.

But there was a voice speaking to me

Awaking the passion so quiet in me, in me, so still in me.

I choose to worship. I just can't give up.

I choose to worship. My mind is made up.

Is that your voice calling me into that secret place with thee.

My heart has longed for this moment with thee.

I choose to worship. I just can't give up.

I choose to worship. My mind is made up."

Many of the people in the church, mostly the black ones, were not familiar with the song that Evelyn was singing, which was, "I Choose To Worship" by Wes Morgan. Be that as it may, they were all enjoying it. As Evelyn was coming to the end of the song, one of the members of the Multimedia Ministry handed the first lady a second, handheld microphone. After sitting out two songs, the first lady led another song.

"Unselfishly died on Calvary

Oh how you gave your life for me

Bruise, scorn, crown your head with thorn, no greater love performed, for me

Nails in Your hands, nails in Your feet, pierced in His side could barely breath,

Could of came down, but yet You remain

177

Standing in awe of the price You paid"

Again, most people weren't familiar with the song First Lady was singing, but they loved it. Evelyn joined her in singing another Wes Morgan song, "You Paid it All."

"I never knew of a love so true

You gave your life and still I hurt you

Lost so many times, crucify you again, but I repent

Forgive me for my sins

You paid it all, up on the cross

You bled and died, 'cause I was lost

So here I am, surrendering all

Lord hear my cry, on my knees I fall

You paid it all, all, you paid it all,

You paid it all, all, you paid it all.

Joanne was at the last few words of "You Paid it All." Evelyn reached back to an old school song, one she was sure everyone in the church knew and would enjoy.

"I feel like going on

Though trials come on every hand

I feel like going on

Feel like going on

Yeah, Yeah"

Joanne joined Evelyn as the two of them sang, "I Feel Like Going On" by Bishop Marvin Winans. Everyone in the church was singing and enjoying the moment.

"I feel like going on

I gotta go - say that I

I feel like going on

The First Lady

Say

Though the storm may be raging

And the billows are tossing high, but

I feel like going on"

As the ladies came to the conclusion of the song, and before they could start a new one, the minister of music began playing something different. Joanne and Evelyn looked at Karen, thinking she was going to sing the song, but quickly realized that wasn't the case. Karen stopped the musician, pointed at Joanne and then Joanne started singing.

"Let the church say amen, let the church say amen

God has spoken, so let the church say amen

Let the church, let 'em say amen

If you believe the word, let the whole church say amen

God has spoken, so let the church say amen

Lift your hands, lift your hands

God has spoken, so let the church say amen,

Oh, thank you Lord

God has spoken, so let the church say amen"

Karen signaled for the musicians to play and the choir to join in on the song.

"Let the church say amen

Let the church...everybody...say amen

God...God has spoken

So let the church...let the church...say...say amen"

Next, Karen gestured for the choir to be quiet and then pointed at Evelyn who began to sing.

"Make this your response...amen

To whatever He says...amen

179

Pastor's Love

From the healing of your body...amen

To the raising of the dead...amen

No matter how you feeling...amen

Or how your world is reeling...amen

Battle on through the night...amen

Cause you're going to win the fight...amen

Even in the valley...amen

Or standing at your red sea...amen

Continue to say...amen

Cause your help is on the way...amen"

The two women hugged one another as they finished the song andthen sent kisses to the minister of music for directing such a great song. To Joanne and Evelyn's surprise, Karen led into another song, accompanied by the musician. This time, Karen pointed to Evelyn to take the lead.

"I had enough heartache and enough headaches

I've had so many ups and downs

Don't know how much more I can take

See, I decided that I cried my last tears yesterday

Either I'm going to trust you or I may as well walk away

'Cause stressing don't make it better

Don't make it better, no way

See, I decided that I cried my last tears yesterday"

Karen indicated for Joanne to join Evelyn; now they were singing jointly.

"Yesterday, yesterday,

I decided to put my trust in you (oh, oh, oh)

Yesterday, yesterday,

I realized that you will bring me through (ah, ah, ah)"

Then Karen signaled for Evelyn to stop and Joanne to continue singing.

"There ain't nothing too hard for my God, no

Any problems that I have

He's greater than them all,

So I decided that I cried my last tear yesterday"

Joanne and Evelyn had just finished their ninth song. Everyone in the church was on their feet applauding. Joanne and Evelyn hugged each other as they stood in the center of the church. During that time, Pastor McCoy stood up and took the podium.

"I hope you all enjoyed the singing and praising as much as I did."

The church expressed joy and happiness.

"I think we should get both of these ladies a singing contract. Please accept my apology for not preaching today. I'm still recovering from the Ironman Triathlon from yesterday, but come back next week; I'll be 100%."

Pastor McCoy said a prayer and ended the noon service. Willie immediately noticed the pastor wasn't taking an offering and there were more than 500 people in the church, which meant an opportunity for a significant offering, perhaps the largest collection in years. While the pastor was praying, Willie got the attention of all the deacons, gathered all of the offering plates and baskets. Then he positioned the deacons by the exit doors so people could leave their offering and or tithes as they exited the church. Everyone slowly departed the church and drove home.

"Babe, I'm tired and hungry. Would you like to stop for a late lunch and early dinner?" Jerome asked Joanne.

"No, I plan on cooking you dinner today. Let's get to the house. You can rest at home while I prepare us a nice dinner."

"No wise man would say no to that."

Jerome and Joanne arrived home and walked inside. Joanne went into the kitchen to quickly inventory what items would be needed for dinner. Jerome entered the large, family room and turned on the large screen, smart television mounted on the wall. Next, he removed his suit coat, tie, dress shirt, shoes, socks, and belt, placing it all on the loveseat as he reclined on the sofa. Joanne left the kitchen and went into the room in which her tired husband was relaxing. She was carrying two large glasses, one of which was sweet tea and the other ice water, as well as two bananas and a bowl of large, red strawberries. Placing everything on the table next to the sofa, Joanne picked up the pastor's clothes and shoes and walked to their bedroom where she slowly put everything away. Then she changed her own clothes.

****

"Kalevi, how are you today; can we talk?" Coleen inquired as she and Sofia approached Kalevi while he walked about in the neighborhood on a Sunday afternoon. Sofia and Coleen knew Demetrius and Kalevi were Joanne's best friends – a gay man and a homeless man. Due to the fact that Demetrius wasn't helping them, they were hoping to obtain some information from Kalevi. Kalevi stopped walking and looked at Coleen and Sofia as they stopped their rental car.

"Hi." Coleen said, Kalevi just looked; he was voiceless when it came to Coleen and Sofia.

"How was service today?" Coleen asked with no reply from Kalevi.

"The pastor preached a good service." There was still no response from Kalevi.

"Are you just going to stare? You're not talking to us, are you mad with us?" Coleen asked, trying to use a seductive voice. Again no reply from Kalevi

"Let's go girl. The military screwed him up, it was stupid

of us to be talking to a homeless and military reject!," Sofia snapped.

"We should get out of this car and kick his ass. I know he'll talk then; he talks to Joanne all the time. Who stole our cars? Is Joanne trying to ruin us?" Coleen asked angrily, receiving no reply from Kalevi.

"This is a waste; let's go girl." Sofia said again.

"I know you can talk and I know you understand us, so you tell that bitch I'm the last bitch she wants as an enemy! You hear me dummy!? Do you hear me retard!? Bye dummy! Coleen shouted as she drove off. Next, Lori pulled up and looked at Kalevi.

"Those your new friends?" Lori asked.

"No, two angry ladies. Not sure why but they're very angry." Kalevi responded in a nonchalant manner and then switched into flirting mode toward Lori.

****

After two hours of cooking and preparing a nice dinner, Joanne walked into the family room and informed her husband that it was dinnertime. Jerome arose from the sofa and then went into the half bathroom next to the family room. After relieving himself, he washed his hands, and walked to the dining room. Once in the dining room, Jerome's eyes widened at what he witnessed – Joanne was standing at the end of the dinner table, which was dressed up fancy. However, Jerome had yet to notice the food on the table. He was mesmerized by his wife's attire which consisted of a one-piece, fitted, sexy piece of lingerie. It stopped halfway between her hips and knees. The garment was designed with mesh that covered her breasts and displayed lots of cleavage. Moreover, it hugged her body, displaying all of her curves and extended her fine, muscular legs in a pair of three inch black shoes.

"Mr. McCoy, for dinner we have filet mignon with mushroom wine sauce, garlic mashed potatoes, and Caesar

salad with your favorite drink, ice tea mixed with ginger ale."
Joanne smiled as she stood at the end of the table in a sexy
pose with her hands on her hips. Jerome walked toward
Joanne as if he was ready to make love. Joanne quickly sat
down at the dinner table.

"Mr. McCoy, your dinner is on the table," said Joanne
with a seductive smile.

"And for dessert?" Jerome was implying she would be his
dessert.

"Your favorite, ice cream – cookies 'n-cream and carrot
cake."

Jerome and Joanne smiled.

"After dessert, I need my pastor to lay his hands on
something. Please have a seat. Your food is getting cold."

Jerome was thinking to himself as he sat down, "I love my
sexy wife."

Chapter Thirteen
Church Planning

"Ladies, unless you provide picture ID, I cannot provide either of you information about an account," the Bank of America customer service representative informed Sofia and Coleen.

Sofia and Coleen arrived at the local Bank of America early Monday morning to check the status of their bank accounts.

"Sir, all of our ID has been stolen, but all we want to know is that our money is still in our account. We're victims of identity theft," Coleen declared.

"Do either of you have a police report. Is there someone here that knows either of you?"

"Sir, please help us! This weekend has been extremely difficult for us; and no, we do not have a police report," Coleen retorted.

"Why?"

"They think we're making it all up," Sofia confessed.

"Sir, please!," Coleen pleaded.

"Ladies, unless you have picture ID, I cannot help. Have you tried to go online and check the status of your account?"

"No sir, we never set up our online account, but we'll do anything for you if you help us." Sofia alluded to sexual favors. However, she was only trying to hustle the bank employee, who called security to come to his desk. Once he arrived, Sofia and Coleen glared at him.

"Ladies, please leave. There's nothing I can do to assist

you." Furious, Sofia and Coleen stood and stormed out of the bank.

"This is crazy, so crazy!," Coleen ranted to Sofia.

"Maybe D is right, we made too many enemies in this city and need to move on. Who knows who's behind all of this," said Sofia.

"I'm not walking away. I have more than a million dollars in that bank, and you talking about just walking away. Not me, you can go, but not me," Coleen stated emphatically.

"Coleen, it's someone with mad computer skills, computer hacking skills. Who do you know with that skill set?" Sofia asked.

"If they're hacking banks, DMV, and our condo unit, they've been arrested by the FBI or some government agency. No one I know."

"Come on, let's ask around. Someone knows someone," Sofia proposed.

****

"Good afternoon saints. Now that we've prayed, sang a song, and read the minutes of the last meeting, I will read the agenda for today's meeting," Sharon Macy, the church clerk announced.

This was the ninth month of Pastor McCoy pastoring Abundant Truth Baptist Church and his third church-wide business meeting. After Pastor McCoy's first business meeting and assembly with the individual ministries, he identified one year goals for the church; which only enraged the good members of the church, as well as the community. They were as follows:

1. Conduct a detailed teaching of spiritual gifts and if necessary, realign members from one ministry to another.

2. Purchase and or acquire the three abandoned

buildings on the block.

3.   Purchase and or obtain the abandoned lots on the block.

4.   Create mission and vision statements for the church and each of the ministries. Also, change the duties and responsibilities of each ministry and put the tasks in writing. Each member of that ministry must sign the agreement (vow to the church members).

5.   Purchase new uniforms for the ushers.

6.   Purchase new uniforms for the culinary ministry.

7.   Provide monthly and quarterly training for all of ministries.

8.   Train or hire someone to be the Youth Pastor.

9.   Create and or update the church's website and other social media outlets.

10. Remodel the church by replacing some of the carpet, remove wallpaper and wooden panel, paint, etc.

Due to the pastor's one year goals list, the people felt he was belittling them and their ability to properly manage church affairs, as well as that they lacked good Bible teaching and had no vision. Members were already angry that he was white; his list of goals only made them hate him even more.

The greatest accomplishment of the church was to own all the property on the block where the church was located. The area consisted of three abandoned buildings and two extremely large, abandoned lots. Now additional problems had been created that the pastor wasn't prepared for. Of course, everyone was looking to Pastor McCoy to fix the problem expediently.

Over the last four to six weeks, the church had been

overflowing with people at the morning and noon services, as well as experiencing a very large increase in tithes and offerings. The main sanctuary could occupy up to 300 people comfortably. Currently, the dining area was being utilized as an overflow room. Furthermore, approximately 100 chairs were placed in the aisles of the church. Church leadership – the Pastor, Deacons, Board of Trustees, and Board of Directors, assumed the overflow was only temporary – a result of Pastor McCoy and Jason competing in the Jacksonville Ironman Triathlon, which was shown throughout the local media and the world with the use of social media outlets. On the other hand, after four weeks, everyone was now assuming the church had quickly increased and it would be the new standard. Therefore, the church had to address the problem immediately. The local news had been reporting that Abundant Truth Baptist Church was growing so fast it would be one of the mega churches in Jacksonville, Florida. They were also predicting that, within two years, it would also become the largest church in Jacksonville, Florida – perhaps, all of Florida.

From its inception in 1940, the population had always been 99% African American and 1% other, such as Hispanics and Latinos, Whites, Cubans, and Puerto Ricans. To date, Abundant Truth Baptist Church was 65% African American, 20% Whites, 5% Hispanics and Latinos, 5% Cubans, and Puerto Ricans and 5% others. It was a rainy, Saturday afternoon and time for the church leadership meeting.

Abundant Truth Baptist Church was getting ready to hold its tri-annual business meeting. On Saturday, the meeting would only consist of individuals in leadership positions; such as members of: the Board of Trustees, Board of Directors, Deacons and Deaconess, President and Vice President of the Ushers, Missionary, Ministry of Music, Health Ministry, Culinary Ministry, as well as the pastor. At the time, the church didn't have associate pastors.

"The agenda has been emailed to everyone, but I will read

over it. The agenda is as follows: overflowing of the church, building of the new church, organizing the church picnic, opening up the doors of the church for new members to join, re-assessing the pastor's salary, cleaning of the lot which including abandoned buildings and empty lots, securing new uniforms for the Ushers and Culinary Ministry and training for the Education Ministry, as well as the need for recruiting people into various ministries. Please note, the meeting will not flow in the order that it was read. If you have anything else on your mind, it may have to wait until the next meeting," Sharon Macy interjected.

"I've placed the agenda in some type of order. However, per the pastor's vision, which I support as well as him, prior to us moving forward, does anyone have questions regarding what's not on the agenda?" Jermaine William, Chairman of the Board of Directors asked as he paused in case anyone had questions.

"Okay, on that note, we will move forward. The first thing is new uniforms for the members of the usher and culinary ministries submitted by the president of those two ministries. The estimated cost is in your package. Any comments?"

"I reviewed the quote submitted; I vote the church pays the full cost of the uniforms and designate them as church property. Via the trustees, the church owns them," said pastor McCoy.

Members of the usher and culinary ministries were very happy with the pastor's response.

Tyrone took out his smart phone and texted all the ushers, "We are getting new uniforms and the church will pay the full price."

Beverly took out her iPad, composing a group email to the four members of the culinary ministry, "We're getting new uniforms, approved by the board. We'll discuss the details soon."

"Thank you Pastor McCoy. Does anyone else have a

comment prior to us voting?"

Everyone in the meeting was quiet. The vote was 100% in favor of Pastor's recommendation.

"Okay, that's it. Sharon, please record it."

"Next, is the cleaning of the lot; I was told that the trustees would like to table the conversation until next week. They're still researching information. Any comments on that?"

Everyone was quiet.

"Okay, on that note, we'll table the topic and move on to the next subject – building of a new church. James, would you speak on that please."

"Good afternoon. About twelve years ago, we researched building a new church when Pastor Paul Carson was here. We have all of the drawings. I met with the architects and builders last week. The plans still work, they just need some updating and then we can build on this lot. What we get with these plans is a one thousand seat sanctuary, full-size kitchen and dining area for 250 people, fifteen offices, twenty classrooms, a full size gym and exercise room, about twenty bathrooms and five showers. Financially, if things stay the same or get better compared to the last four weeks, we can pay off the church within three years, and that's with 25% down, which is currently 75% of what we have in the bank," James reported to the Chairman of the Board of Trustees.

"Any comments prior to the vote?" Jermaine asked.

Tyrone stood up and expressed, "We're averaging more than 500 people attending the noon service. By the time the new building is built, it could be too small."

"I agree with Tyrone!," Willie shouted. He was chairman of the deacons.

James stood and said, "We can add a U-shaped balcony; which will add an additional 500 seats with very little changes to the blueprints."

"I recommend we wait until James has a chance to meet with the builders and architects again to discuss the idea of adding additional seats, then brief the whole church next week," Jermaine suggested.

"I'm okay with that recommendation," said Pastor McCoy. "But I do have a question."

"Yes, Pastor," James replied.

"There are some homeless people living in the abandoned building. I recommend we develop a plan for them prior to any construction on this site."

"James, has your team considered that?" Willie asked.

"No," James answered.

Everyone in the church was quiet.

"James, is that something your team can research and brief the church next week?" Jermaine asked.

"Not a problem, we'll take the lead and have a few ideas next week."

"Thank you. Are there any other questions for James?" Jermaine queried. "Okay, next on the agenda. Opening the doors of the church for people to join, this is for you Pastor McCoy. To give you a little history, prior to your arrival, we opened the doors of the church every Sunday. Since you've been here, it hasn't happened in about nine months now. Many of us have been told by those visiting that they would love to join the church. If possible, can you address that concern?"

"First, please accept my apology for not opening the doors of the church. I will do it tomorrow for sure. However, I would like to recommend that we open the doors for new members once a month, not weekly, but I'm open to ideas," said Pastor McCoy.

"I can live with once a month. Would anyone like to comment on that?" Jermaine asked.

"I'm happy with opening the doors of the church once a month," Willie responded.

Everyone else remained silent.

"Finally, let's discuss the pastor's salary. I'm not sure who asked for this, but I don't see a problem with the pastor's salary. Does anyone disagree?"

No one uttered a word.

"I know nothing about this," said James, the Trustee.

"It's new to me as well," said Willie.

"I asked for it." Barbara Long, Co-chairman of the Board of Directors spoke up.

"Barbara, can you elaborate a little for us all?" Jermaine requested.

"I know whatever is collected on fourth Sunday is the pastor's salary. However, last month we wrote a check for more than sixty thousand dollars. The way things are looking, it will be the same this month and increasing monthly."

"Barbara, I talked to the Deacons and Deaconess about this prior to the meeting, and I don't understand your concern," Willie, Chairman of the Deacons challenged.

"Mr. Chairman, when pastor arrived, his salary was basically five thousand dollars a month. Now we're looking at sixty thousand dollars a month. His salary increased from sixty thousand annually to more than seven hundred thousand dollars a year. Am I the only one who sees a problem with this salary? He's not working more hours."

Everyone saw the stress in Barbara.

"The contract agreement which had been the same for roughly thirty or more years now, clearly states the pastor's salary is the total amount collected every 4th Sunday. How many hours he works has no value to his salary," Willie challenged.

"Then again, the expectation is that pastor will work a full 40 hour week," James asserted.

"Well, speak your mind and let's put it to a vote," Jermaine countered.

"I would like to know what pastor thinks about it?" Barbara said.

"No, it's time to vote," Jermaine interjected.

"I don't mind speaking," Pastor McCoy interjected.

"No need to speak pastor. When you arrived, you accepted the salary and the agreement. We signed a contract; now we the church, need to remain true to what we agreed on," James, Chairman of the Trustees expressed.

"This is not NATO. Interpretations are not needed nor permitted here. Will you all let the man speak, please, Barbara reprimanded.

"She'll be getting a visitor this week," said Tyrone, President of the Ushers to Charlene, President of the Health Ministry, and Beverly, President of the Culinary Ministry.

"From who?" Charlene and Beverly asked the question in unison.

"Wow, it's like that now? Both of you know who. She'll be singing a different tune in a few days, just watch."

"Barbara, you'll meet the first lady soon," Charlene and Beverly said to themselves.

"Barbara, out of respect, please address pastor properly, not as 'that man'," Willie the Chairman of the Deacons cautioned her.

"Pastor, my church family, please accept my apology. But I would like to hear from pastor without everyone else speaking on his behalf; this is not a courtroom. I feel like if we start paying pastor sixty thousand dollars a month, his salary will be over seven hundred thousand dollars a year. I think everyone in the church would agree that's too much money.

After all, how much did they pay Jesus?"

"I will share my thoughts with you all," replied Pastor McCoy as he stood to his feet.

"No, I was hoping the first lady would get her." Tyrone said to himself using his inner voice.

"Thank you Pastor but the more I think about it, I think we should talk about this next week, during the church-wide business meeting," Barbara recanted.

"That was a foolish move, Barbara. Now you have to deal with the first lady," Tyrone thought to himself.

"Stupid," Jerome, Willie and Jermaine was thinking to themselves about Barbara

"I'm okay with talking about it next week as well," Pastor McCoy consented.

"Pastor, this is not necessary. We can and should put this to rest now," James spoke up.

"I agree," echoed Willie and Jermaine in unison.

"I'm okay with whatever Sister Barbara feels comfortable with," Pastor McCoy countered.

"Next week is best for me and the whole church," Barbara communicated as she retired to her seat, smiling and feeling happy.

"Next week it is; I'm fine with that," Pastor McCoy stated.

"Well, this concludes our meeting today. Chairman, can you close us out with a prayer?" Jermaine asked reluctantly.

Willie Long, Chairman of the Deacons, closed the meeting with a prayer. Seconds later, everyone started texting, talking, and exiting the church.

"Barbara, I really wish we had discussed your concerns before today's meeting." James McDonald, Chairman of the Trustees conveyed as he and Barbara stood in the parking lot with as the hot sun dried up the early morning rain shower.

"Mr. Chairman, I've watched people in this church change a lot since the pastor arrived. I do not understand the hold he has on the people here; people are changing. We were a nice, friendly, community family church; now look at us, just a bunch of yes man to him."

"What are you talking about?" James asked looking dumbfounded as it related to Barbara's perception. "Things have improved 100 times over since the pastor arrived."

"He shouldn't be getting paid no sixty thousand dollars a month – sixty thousand a year, yes, but not a month."

"Barbara, do you know how many pastors turned down the position because of the salary?"

"None, we only offered it to one person."

"Correction, Ms. Sherlock Holmes. During the interview, all, about twenty of them said they would not accept the position with such low salary for a full-time position. Out of the twenty, only three had a Bachelor's degree. Pastor McCoy was the only one with a Doctoral degree."

"James, I like the pastor's teaching and preaching. He is truly anointed as well as the first lady, but he's not worth sixty thousand dollars a month. We're a community church; most of the people in the church or the community make that much money a year."

"Barbara, wake up! While you were watching the money and the pastor's salary, you failed to notice we're not a community church anymore. Blacks still make up 90% of the community, but we're about 65% of this church; 35% are other ethnicities and its steadily changing each Sunday. Soon we'll be 50% or less. Do you think the blacks in this community are contributing all of that money every Sunday? Prior to Pastor McCoy, we were doing good to get six thousand dollars on a Sunday, and that included two services. We have a sanctuary designed to hold three hundred people. Yet, we were only averaging 50 to 75. Look at us now, we're the talk of the town, the fastest growing church in the state."

"So what! What does that mean?"

"Barbara, if we collect $60,000 four times a month, and give Pastor one of those Sunday offerings as his income, that's still $180,000 for the church in one month. Prior to him coming here, that's more than what we received in one year."

"So what; his salary is too much."

"I believe a growing church is blessed from the Lord Jesus. One that's not growing is not cursed, but receiving no blessings."

"The people will speak next week James. If I'm wrong, we'll know next week."

"Barbara, little do you know, you'll be singing a different tune next week." James was referring to an impromptu meeting between Barbara and Joanne and Barbara reversing her viewpoint as many others had.

"What do you mean?"

"Next week, you have a good day and enjoy yourself." Then James walked away.

Outside the church, everyone was watching as Joanne rode into the parking lot and parked her Harley-Davidson next to her husband's Harley. They had two motorcycles each. She took off her helmet and patiently waited for her husband to come out of the church. Seconds later, the pastor walked out of the church and up to his wife and gave her a big juicy kiss.

"Look at those bikes. They're probably worth thirty thousand dollars each," Barbara said to Charlene and Beverly.

"And?" Charlene countered.

"Is it just I!? Does anyone see a problem with the salary we're paying the pastor?"

"Barbara, those bikes came with them from Washington. Did you know the First Lady has a chain of hair salons on the West Coast?" Tyrone inquired.

"Wrong Detective Dick Tracy, she has a cosmetology license, but she doesn't own a hair salon. I read the investigator report myself." Barbara smirked as if to say, I got this.

"Sure thing, bye," Tyrone replied as he walked away.

Jermaine and Willie were walking out to their car and started approaching Barbara. "Willie and Jermaine, I have a question for you two. What do you think about the First Lady being a bike rider?"

"Not sure of your question," Willie replied.

"It doesn't look ladylike, especially with her being the First Lady of the church."

"Have a nice day," Willie said to Jermaine as they continued to their cars then drove away.

****

"Now there you are in the midst of the storm with the Lord Jesus and He does nothing about it. Better yet, He's sleeping while you're going through the storm. Picture that, the Lord Jesus is with you while you're in the midst of a storm. Your life is in question and the Lord Jesus does not help, and He has the audacity to go to sleep with a pillow while you're fighting for your life."

Everyone in the church was quiet; Pastor McCoy was preaching at the noon service; he also preached at the morning service. The pastor had been preaching now for the past twenty minutes. He was closing up his message for the day. His topic was, "Jesus is Waiting on You to Call on Him;" the day's scripture was from Mark 4:35-41.

"I'm not making this up. It's in my Bible, check your Bible as well. Here it is, Mark 4:36–they enter a ship and smaller ships are with them; verse 37 – a great wind, the waves beat into the ship; verse 38 – Jesus sleeping, sleeping with a pillow; and the people in fear of their lives. Now here in verse 39, after the people awaken Jesus, after they called on

Jesus, He responded. I'm telling you Abundant Truth, the Lord Jesus is with you in your troubles. But unless you faithfully call on Him, He will not respond. I'm telling you to call him in the morning, day, and night, call on the Lord Jesus at all times. He is with you and waiting to hear from you."

Everyone in the church jumped to their feet, applauding and shouting amen and Jesus.

"The doors of the church are open. If you desire to become a member of this church, the doors of the church are open. Walk toward the altar, give the deacons your hand and your heart to the Lord Jesus," Pastor McCoy encouraged.

Approximately 200 people came forward to join, just as many joined at the morning service. The deacons and deaconesses collected information from the new members and then the pastor closed out the noon service.

****

"There she is!" Coleen exclaimed to Sofia, as they both watched Joanne exit the church and start her drive home.

"What's on your mind?" Sofia inquired.

"We should talk to her – just talk."

"No, I'm getting out; I'm not down with this," Sofia refused.

"What!"

"Demetrius is right; we made a lot of enemies in this town. We should have left two years ago when he suggested it. He was right."

"Come on, we're just gonna talk,"Coleen urged as she and Sofia followed Joanne in a rental car.

"Coleen, think about it, we destroyed a lot of families. We hustled a lot of retirement and college funds, couples divorced, and the pay offs – just let me out!" Coleen stopped following Joanne, pulled the car over to the side of the street, parked then glared at Sofia.

"So what do we do?"

"You go talk to her, but not with me."

"We're girls. I have no one else in this world; I don't want to lose you. What do we do now? We're broke, no car, no home, no job, nothing; what do we do now?"

"We talk to Demetrius. We relocate our hustle, maybe out West or Atlanta, Georgia."

"Demetrius, wow, let's go!"

****

"Ladies I'm surprised to see you two talking to each other," Barbara said to Joanne McCoy and Valerie Coleman, her accountant as an expression of disbelief came over her.

It was Thursday and Barbara was on her way to Valerie's office for a meeting to discuss the extension of her current business. Valerie was a white female and had been managing Barbara's books as her accountant for the past ten years. Barbara was the owner of twelve strip clubs located from northern Jacksonville to Orlando, Florida. The names of the clubs ranged from Juicy, Dicks, GC, Topless, The Blue Moon, Bottoms, and The Bush Company.

Ten years prior, Barbara's ex-husband, Danny Power, died. Barbara and their only child, Darlene, who was only six months old at the time, jointly inherited six strip clubs. Over the years, Barbara noticed how easy it was to manage a nightclub; as well as how much money there was to make. She extended the business from six to twelve clubs. With the help of Valerie, she managed to keep everything in her dead, ex-husband's name while she and her daughter lived a very comfortable and wholesome life in Jacksonville, Florida.

Barbara stopped at a local coffee shop located down the street from Valerie's office. She entered the coffee shop to kill time and enjoy a nice sandwich and a cup of coffee. As she approached the counter to place her order, she noticed Valerie and Joanne talking and laughing; which caused her jaws to drop. She wondered why they were talking. More so, were they talking about her? If they were, how much had Valerie shared with Joanne and what were the chances of her keeping her business private, as she had for the past 10 years? Now Barbara was on the hunt to know what Joanne knew about her.

"Barbara, we grew up in the same neighborhood in South Seattle, Washington. When I was home last month, I was told Joanne had moved out this way, so we're just catching up with each other," Valerie explained.

"Really!," Barbara yelped, thinking she was screwed.

"You two have something in common."

"Like what?" Barbara asked in a tone that caused Valerie and Joanne to raise their eyebrows.

"Joanne owns a chain of salons located in Washington State, Oregon, and Northern California. I think about twenty-one in total. They're the upscale ones. And you…"

Before Valerie could say another word, Barbara interrupted.

"You know…Let me leave you ladies to catch up. Are we are still on schedule to meet in about a half hour?"

"Yes, see you soon."

Barbara walked out of the coffee shop without ordering a drink. She was attempting to figure out how to approach Valerie and or Joanne; she was concerned about members of the church and the community learning about her business – the owner of several nudist clubs that exploited young females.

Joanne and Valerie finished their conversation and went their separate ways. Valerie agreed to visit the church soon.

****

"Saints, may I have your attention please. We have a lot of information to relay today, so let's get started," said Willie at the church-wide business meeting.

Pastor McCoy had opened the meeting with a prayer. Sharon had read the minutes from the previous meeting and the agenda of today's meeting, and then she handed things over to Jermaine.

"Okay, everyone was given a handout on today's meeting. I would like someone from the trustees to come forward and explain the church picnic and the construction of the new church."

James, Chairman of the Trustees, walked forward and spoke. "As many of you know, approximately twenty years ago, we researched the idea of building a new church. For several reasons, it was not the proper time. Fortunately, our time has arrived; now is the time. We have updated the blueprints and they're on display in the dining area and hallways for everyone to see. The new church will be built in the center of this block. We'll be able to use this building until the new church is completed. Afterwards, this building will be demolished and the space used for additional parking. Construction can begin in about sixty days. Costwise, I'm recommending we pay 25% now, which is roughly 75 to 90% of what we have in the two banks. Based on what we've been collecting over the last four to six weeks, we should be able to pay off the church in less than three years. That's without selling chicken dinners, sweet potato pies, or having a building fund."

Everyone laughed.

"In addition, we can start getting the lot and block cleaned off and prepared as soon as next week. I propose we hold the church's annual picnic here, the Saturday before the start of construction on Monday."

"As far as the overflow of people, I kicked the idea around with pastor and he's onboard, which is to add a third Sunday service. He will preach at two of the services and the associate pastors in training will preach once a Sunday and be paid a fee."

"Does anyone have any questions about the new church, the picnic, or adding a third service to reduce the crowd in the morning and noon services?"

Three people raised their hands. Jermaine pointed to a young lady in the back.

"Oh," shouted James before the young lady started speaking. "Excuse me Chairman but I forgot something. Lori, who works in my office downtown with the city and is a member of the church, shared an idea with me. The idea, is, there is a large, six level building, an old hotel about two blocks away, some of you know what I'm talking about. It's been abandoned for more than six years and the taxes are behind. Lori did some research; she's not here today to explain, but according to city and state laws, the city can sell that building for the back taxes, which are about $44,000. Lori also stated that the new owner of the building would also qualify for state and federal grants for repairs, as well as a low interest rate loan.

Last week, pastor asked a question about the homeless people in the abandoned building on this block that will be demolished for the new church. Well, here's my idea, the church can purchase the old hotel, and restore it to a livable condition to be used as a homeless shelter. We should be able to get other churches in the city to partner with us. Also, according to Lori, if we use it for a homeless shelter, we would be eligible to receive $10 per day from the city, $21 per day from the state, and $45 per day from the federal government, totaling $76 per person, per night for homeless individuals who reside there. She also believes we would gain support from the community, local businesses, as well as other churches. With the exception of the initial investment, the homeless building should be able to support itself."

"James, who do you suppose would manage the property?" Willie asked.

"My initial guess is the building becomes property of the church, which would be the responsibility of the trustees. The

Missionary board would also have a hand in managing the building. Lori has agreed to write all the grants; she does that now for the city and is extremely proficient at her job."

"Okay, sounds good. Let's move on to questions; you have the floor now." Jermaine addressed the lady who was up to speak prior to James's interruption.

"Why do you think we should spend 75 to 90% of the church's saving on a new building? I'm thinking if something goes wrong, which a million things could, we lose 75 to 90% of the church's capital."

"I agree, sister. It may sound risky, but we all know nothing is guaranteed. Currently, what's in the church's savings account has been accumulating over the past thirty years. If the church continues to grow as it has in the past eight weeks, we'll be able to pay off the new building plus replenish the savings, all in three years. My plan is half of what we collect on Sundays will go toward the new building and the other half in the bank. Therefore, the initial investment should be recovered in less than a year. Do you have any other questions?"

"No."

Jermaine pointed to another lady in the middle.

"If we do three services, what will the times be?"

"I'm not sure. We have to get with the pastor. Presently, we're doing service at 8:00 and 11:30a.m. So my thoughts are something like 2:00 or 3:00p.m. Do you have other questions?"

"No."

Jermaine pointed to a man in the back.

"Two questions; will the third service work as far as reducing the overflow problem and how long will it take to build the new church?"

"First answer, we're hoping the third service will work. I

think if the pastor preaches at the 8:00 a.m. And 2:00 p.m. services, it would balance the number of people across all three services. Maybe we should survey the church. In response to your second question, the construction will take approximately 18 to 24 months, but I think we'll be able to occupy it for Sunday service after 9 to 12 months. This building will be used for everything else, but we should be able to utilize the new 1,500 seat sanctuary soon. I know last week we discussed a 1,000 seat sanctuary, but the architect and builder confirmed we can add the balcony without making major changes or incurring additional expenses. That revision alone will provide another 500 seats. Do you have another question?"

"No."

"Does anyone else have questions?"

Everyone was quiet. James walked to his seat then Jermaine stood up to speak.

"Okay, we'll be voting on three things very soon, but we have one more item to discuss which is Pastor's salary. Barbara Power, Vice President of the Trustees, please come forward and address the members," Jermaine requested and then sat down.

Barbara stood up slowly. She was acting as if she was confused about her whereabouts and what to say, but she made her way to the front of the church with everyone looking on.

"A worker is worthy of his wages. I think our Pastor is a great laborer in the Lord Jesus, as well as the church and community. Thereby, worthy of whatever compensation he receives. I'm happy with Pastor's salary and hope everyone else is as well. Let us applaud our Pastor for laboring for the Lord Jesus, for being our Pastor, and for his leadership and vision."

Everyone in the church stood and clapped their hands; Barbara walked back to her seat. Tyrone looked at Charlene and Beverly. You had a special visit by the first lady. I know, I received one as well, they thought to themselves.

Strangely, Jermaine looked at James as they both hunched their shoulders as if to say, I don't know what happened.

"Okay, voting time," Jermaine announced.

The members voted, the pastor closed the meeting with a prayer, and then everyone left the church slowly.

****

"Babe, you okay? You looked at that man as if you were looking at a ghost. What's wrong?" Jerome asked Joanne, as the couple exited their car and strolled toward Marker 32 for dinner.

"Your father always told me to be aware of Chinese people."

"My father is a paranoid man. He believes the Chinese are destroying this country and others; he always voted Democratic, but I really think he's a Republican. Jerome jokingly smiled.

"Well, he may be paranoid, but I've seen that same Chinese man three times in the past week and at three different locations. That's extremely odd."

"Well he'll be here soon. You can talk to him; he's coming out to celebrate my birthday and our first year in Jacksonville."

"Good!" Joanne responded as she glanced behind her at the two Chinese men they had just passed.

****

"I think she noticed you," Bai said to Jian, the two men were members of the Ministry of State Security (MSS); they were sent to Jacksonville to gather information on Jerome McCoy.

"I don't see how," Jian replied.

"The way she looked at you was not good and it's not worth the risk; return to the Embassy tonight."

"And you?"

"I will ask for a replacement for you, but Beijing is sending an interrogation and death squad to the city. They will be coming into the country via Canada within a few days."

"He's a simple pastor; we can handle it."

"Beijing has decided."

****

Joanne's cell phone whistled; it was a text message from Demetrius, "Call me now!"

"Babe, I'm going to the restroom, I'll be back in a few minutes." Joanne left her husband at the dinner table, went into the ladies restroom, and called Demetrius from her cell phone.

"D, I'm having dinner with my husband. What's up?"

"I'm at Kaluby's Banquet Ballroom making reservations for your husband's surprise birthday party, August 20st, 250 people, at $125.00 per person, including finger food from 5:00 to 6:30 p.m. Dinner will be a seafood and steak buffet from 6:30 to 8:30 p.m. and an open bar all night. You'll have the place from 5:00 p.m. to midnight. Do you want me to sign the contract and give them the deposit?"

"Yes, let's push the number up to 300 people."

"Your money; bye."

"Bye." Joanne returned to her table for dinner

Chapter Fourteen

Confession

"Last night, he came to my home. Reluctantly, I got in the car with him. We were going to his house, but he stopped at a park. He was forcing himself on me, touching my body and kissing me. I tried to get away but he was chasing me; I was scared so I shot and killed him," Evelyn confided in Joanne.

Joanne noticed Evelyn crying during Bible study, so afterwards, she went over and sat beside Evelyn and hugged her. Travis was sitting a few pews behind them. He sat and watched as the First Lady and Evelyn talked.

"Start from the beginning so I can understand it all, please."

"Jason is gone for the week. Carroll has been calling me for weeks and coming to my home uninvited. Last night, he wouldn't leave. He was forcing himself into my home. I know it was not going to be a good night. He kept telling me how much he loved me and how I was going to be his lady. He wouldn't leave. I asked could we go to his place instead. I locked up my home and got into his car. As we were driving, he stopped for drinks, which was strange because he has a full bar at his home fully stock with various types of alcohol.

While he was in the store, I removed his gun from his glove compartment. Then he drove to Metropolitan Park, and told me we were just going to talk under the moonlight and enjoy a nice drink in the park. He started kissing and touching me, placing my hand on his private parts; it all made me sick. I pushed him and started running away. I fell down and saw him coming. So I started shooting. When he fell, I got up and started running again. Next thing I know, I was walking on Talleyrand Ave. Then Travis came out of nowhere and offered me a ride home."

Joanne turned around and spotted Travis sitting behind them. She smiled at Travis and then refocused her attention on Evelyn.

"Where's the gun?"

"I have it with me."

"What do you want to do?"

"I'm afraid. I don't want to go to jail. Can you help me?"

"Can you handle killing someone and walking away?"

"Carroll has friends and enemies; they will either be extremely happy or extremely angry. I'm scared."

Joanne took a deep breath. She had read about the murder of Carroll Benson in the morning newspaper. However, what she read was not supported by what Evelyn had just told her.

"Give me the gun," Joanne stated.

Evelyn handed Joanne a gun that was wrapped in a small towel.

"Go home and relax," Joanne instructed.

Evelyn got up and went to the bathroom and then Travis walked up to Joanne.

"I can dispose of that for you, Ms. First Lady McCoy. This matter has history; there is no need to get your hands dirty. Give it to me and return to your husband," Travis ordered with a serious expression on his face, one that Joanne had never noticed.

Joanne looked at Travis. She heard the rumors of Krystal, Travis's wife, and Carroll. She noticed the intense look on Travis's face. Eventually, she handed him the towel-wrapped gun and walked away. Travis placed the towel and gun in a plastic bag; he spotted Evelyn leaving the church, heading into the parking lot. Travis walked at a fast pace to catch up with her. When he reached Evelyn, she gave him her million dollar smile although she was in pain internally. Travis was especially happy that Evelyn's reaction was welcoming and inviting. Both of them stood by Evelyn's car.

"Last night, I came to your home to ask you out for dinner. When I arrived, I saw you getting in the car with Carroll Benson; you didn't look happy. I followed the two of you and watched him park his car in the parking lot off of Festival Park Ave. Then I quickly parked my truck off of E. Bay Street, ran back, and watched you two in the park. I saw you running and him chasing you then I watched you fall and was surprised to see you shoot at him then run out of the park. Your shot grazed his forehead.

I went up to him and placed two shots in the back of his head. Evelyn, he killed my wife. I could handle her leaving me and the children to be with him, but having my wife was not enough for him. He took my job, my home, my savings, and killed my daughters' mother then disposed of her as if she were trash. To add insult to injury, the city officials – the mayor's office and JPD didn't investigate. For years, Carroll punked this city and its officials. Someone had to say enough, but that's not why I killed him. He's dead because I love you and was afraid he would take you from me. He would have killed you as well. I hope one day you can love me as well, and we become as one." By now, tears were rapidly streaming down both Evelyn and Travis' face.

"What are they talking about?" Jerome asked Joanne.

"She thinks she killed Carroll Benson last night."

"She thinks, but you think not?"

"The newspaper reported he was shot twice in the back of the head. According to her story, if she killed him, he should have been shot in the front of the head."

"And why do you believe her?"

"I think I know who did it."

"What…What are you talking about!?" Jerome asked.

"I think she's talking to the killer now, and he's telling her that."

"I thought you said they have the murder weapon."

"That's what the media reported. The murder weapon was found next to his body. I'm confident they'll find the prints of Carroll Benson and or Krystal McKnight," Joanne declared.

"Really?"

"Love kills. I think Travis saved that weapon for years for this moment. Once he was convinced that the faith of Evelyn was going to be the same as Krystal's, the decision to kill Carroll became apparent and was effortless."

"Let's go home, Ms. Detective."

"Look at that."

Evelyn and Travis were kissing in the parking lot. Jerome and Joanne drove home.

****

"Boss, we identified the Chinamen following Joanne and Jerome. They are members of MSS," Wendy reported to Neo.

"I know, Beijing is sending an interrogation and death squad to the area. A team from DC has been deployed to Canada to stop them if possible," Neo replied.

"And if they fail?"

"We will deal with it in Jacksonville," Neo answered.

"What's your status?"

"Making preparation for a road trip. I'm heading to the area soon. They plan to take him or kill the entire family on the anniversary day."

"Do you know the date?"

"August 20th, the day before Jerome's birthday."

"And how do you know this?"

"It's the anniversary date of the Chinese Embassy bombing in Africa."

****

"Ladies, I know you two don't have an appointment. What can I do for you today?" Demetrius said to Coleen and Sofia as they entered his salon; which was located on the Northern side of town.

"We decided to take your advice and leave town," Sofia responded.

"Today, now?" Demetrius asked.

"Yes. Like you said, we've hustled this town enough and made numerous enemies," Coleen replied.

"Unfortunately, we're broke – no car, no home, no nothing, someone took it all," Sofia added.

"You should have listened to me. Two years ago, you both had a lot more." Demetrius criticized as he walked to his carrying bag which was in a chair. He removed two envelopes and handed one to each of them.

****

"This is a nice picnic, everything looks nice." Calvin said to Willie.

This was the church's annual picnic. Normally, it was held in one of the local parks, but on this day it was taking place on the lot that the church owned. It was a huge success. Hundreds of people attended the picnic. Everyone was enjoying themselves. The interaction between Travis and Evelyn's family, as if they were one family was noticed by many. Kalevi and Lori were being watched also, but they had no children.

There were three, large tents set-up in a u-shape. In the

middle tent were fifty tables with various board games such as: Chess, Scrabble, Checkers, Monopoly, Uno, Bingo, Bible Trivia, etc. The tents on both sides of the middle tent had seating – tables and chairs for 250 people for eating and relaxing. In front of the middle tent were four, large grills full of food and a smaller tent with five tables full of food.

The pastor and first lady; as well as many others, were having a great time with lots of conversation and game-playing taking place.

"Pastor wants to hire two additional pastors. One will be the youth pastor and the other an associate pastor and he wants to pay them out of his salary," Willie, Chairman of the Deacons, told Jermaine, Chairman of the Board of Directors.

"Yes, we talked about it briefly last week. I think he tapped Calvin Green to be the youth pastor," Jermaine shared.

"Calvin is a good man. He has a good wife and family, but I didn't see that coming," Willie divulged.

"He talked to you about their salary?" Jermaine asked.

"Fifteen thousand dollars a month from his salary to be used to pay their salaries. One will get sixty thousand dollars a year and the other something like seventy-five thousand dollars," Willie disclosed.

"Good, it's needed in order to grow. Do you think he'll miss the money?" Jermaine speculated.

"No! The first lady is rich and he's already receiving speaking engagements at other churches, colleges, and large businesses. He's been turning down all of the invitations but once people offer more, he'll accept. Then he'll earn about ten to twenty-five thousand dollars per engagement. The man is extremely smart," Willie acknowledged.

"Wow, why not me! You know his wife is giving him a surprise birthday party. Rumor has it that she spent fifty thousand dollars on it."

"She has class. You must admit, our First Lady has class," Willie admitted.

****

"Kalevi and Lori, good afternoon. How are you two?" Joanne greeted.

"We're well." Both Lori and Kalevi answered.

"And thanks for the invite to Pastor's birthday party," Lori expressed.

"You're both welcome. May I have a minute with Kalevi, please?"

"Kalevi, I'm going to get those hamburgers off the grill; I'll see you soon," Lori stated as she walked away, leaving Kalevi and Joanne to talk in private.

"Brother Kalevi, there's a rumor that I would like to share with you."

Kalevi looked at Joanne, wondering what she was talking about.

"And!"

"The rumor goes like this, about three days prior to your graduation from high school, the CIA, FBI, DIA, ONI, NSA and every other three letter government agency in this country kicked your parents' doors down and arrested you for hacking into the U.S. Government and many other foreign government's most secured systems. Because you refused to work for the government as a hacker, the President of the United States ordered you into the U.S. Marine Corps. After spending eight to ten years in the military with an outstandingly successful record, you woke up not talking or knowing your name or location. After a year of evaluation, the military medically discharged you. Then you returned to Jacksonville and started living life as a homeless man. How am I doing with the rumors?"

Kalevi grinned, but said nothing.

"The rumor gets better. Some people think your sudden medical dilemma was a ploy to get out of the military and keep government agencies off your back. Genius! Working the government, making them think you were mentally challenged. Harvard even has terminology for it; remind me to look it up for you one day. Congratulations! Any words for me?"

Kalevi simply smiled.

"A few days ago, more than three million dollars arrived at the church from an anonymous donor with a note attached that said it was to be used for the homeless only. It also provided the location of furniture in a local storage unit that was also only to be used for the homeless ministry. Any comment?"

Kalevi remained silent, smiling he realized that Joanne knew too much about him and his clandestine activities.

"Kalevi, I'm not going to ask if you broke the law by hacking into someone's account or business and eradicated the resources of our friends, Sofia and Coleen. However, I am telling you this; I must know your illegal activities are behind you. You cannot be the pastor's armor-bearer and remain close to him if you're breaking the law. He must be protected."

Kalevi was confused; he heard the rumors about Joanne being a bully and a thug. Therefore, he was surprised by what she was saying.

"Kalevi, I'm waiting on you," Lori said a few feet away, heading to a chair and table to enjoy her burger.

"I need to leave; my friend is waiting on me."

"Kalevi," Joanne stated in a firm, clear voice. Kalevi noticed the tone of her voice had changed. "Please answer my question, now!"

Kalevi loved the first lady and pastor; he wanted to do the right thing.

"Do the name Jeffery Wright, mean anything to you?"

"No, why?"

"What about Samuel Black?"

"No, why!" Joanne replied with a touch of attitude in the tone of her voice. She was having an intense conversation with someone she liked and respected and did not want to damage their relationship, but she loved her husband and wanted him to be very successful. "Please tell me Kalevi why I should know the two of them."

"You saw them, you met them, you talked to them, but you do not know them, what a surprised, Ms. First Lady," Kalevi said with a little sarcasm in his voice

Joanne was taken by surprised by Kalevi choice of words and puzzled as to how to reply, but she knew the characteristic of the first lady and what her mother taught her.

"What do Mr. Black and Mr. Wright have to do with our conversation and you hacking to secured networks and removing the digital life of two individuals?"

"One father, two mothers, two brothers, two families, two hustlers, the same story. Mr. Lawrence Black was once a successful businessman in the medical supplies field, with more than 10,000 employees around the world. Mr. Robert Wright owned an Information Technology company with about 2,500 employees in the state of Florida, Georgia, Virginia and DC. with government contracts all over the country. Their father is dead, their mothers were dying from cancer. Both brothers with a wife and three children and living the American dream. With all of their flaws and medical challenges they were still living the dream. Mr. Black a wife, three children, two sons and daughter. The daughter attending Brown University, you know any thing about Brown University?" Kalevi looks at Joanne from a side eye view.

"Ivy League college located in Providence, in Rhode Island."

"Yes, you know, one son in high school and the other son, home dealing with Parkinson Disease, I think. Mr. Wright, the same a wife, one son and two daughters; one son in college, University of Miami, one still in high school and his daughter home with Cerebral Palsy. You see where these stories are going?"

"Please educate me."

"The hustlers, hustle the men out of everything, money for their mother's medical bill, their children's college educational funds, company payroll, employees 401K. They bankrupted their company by taking the ladies on expensive trips and buying them luxury items. Without the brothers knowing it, the ladies gained control of their bank accounts and accounts to everything and place money existed. Before you knew it, the brothers were in court being sued by their clients, and slowly with lawsuits and legal fees, no money for college, no more nice home, nice car, no money for medical bills. Their children turned to drugs, their mothers died, the ones with Cerebral Palsy and Parkinson died, the ones on drugs died due to an overdose."

Tears were in Joanne's eyes

"Do not cry on me first lady, you started down this road, now we are here. One son survived from both families, and they teamed up to find the hustlers that caused the death of their loved ones. Well, after years of looking the taste for revenge deserted both men. Then one day, you asked me to invite my homeless homies to church and after one visit to Abundant Truth Baptist Church, the taste to kill resurfaced and it rested on the tip of the tongues of both men."

"What!"

"Yes, different names, but the same ladies."

"Whatever you may think, my hacking and illegal activities saved those two ladies their lives. I promised my roommates its best to attack them in the digital world and allow them to live, instead of killing them and maybe going to prison. So, they lived today, with the pain of losing it all, and the lone survivor from each family has enough money to start a new life."

"Thank you," Joanne said with a smile and tears in her eyes as she looked over to Kalevi's two roommates sitting, eating and enjoying themselves at the church annually cookout, without a worry in the world.

"But know, my illegal hacking business is over."

Joanne reached over and hugged Kalevi, then the both of them turned around and walked into different directions.

"Thank you. Please enjoy your day." Kalevi walked away and towards Lori and Joanne reunited with her husband.

****

"Yes sir." Kang Hsieh answered the secured phone in his office in the Chinese Embassy in Washington, D.C.

"I'm sending two teams. One is a death squad and the other an interrogation team. They will enter the country from Canada. Their shopping list is in your email. Please give them all the support they need." Located in Beijing, Ming-hug Yu, the Director of Ministry of State Security requested.

"Sir, the match was only 75%, and all the data gathered and analyzed tells us he's not our man. Why the two teams?"

"I believe he's the son of Robert Sammy Johnson and will lead us to either his father or his father's partner, Richard Turner. If either man is still alive, it proves the U.S. has misled us for more than thirty years and one of the two men is responsible for our embassy bombings from 1981 through 1988. If so, we need to bring them to China for trial."

"Thank you sir, goodbye," Kang Hsieh replied.

***

"What is this?" Sofia asked.

"It showed up in my mailbox a few days ago. I have no

clue what's in it or where it came from," Demetrius replied. Sofia and Coleen opened the envelopes. Each envelope contained $5,000 in cash and a one-way bus trip to any place in the U.S.

"Someone is telling us to get out of town and leave now!," Coleen snapped with a smile. "We've been hustled.

****

"Do you feel like you've been blackmailed by the first lady?" Charlene asked Beverly.

Charlene was still upset that Joanne got the best of her many months ago. Her husband, Richard, told her to stay away from the first lady, but Charlene refused to accept defeat. As a matter of fact, she believed that with her Doctoral degree, she should be much smarter than someone with a hair license degree.

"What are you talking about?" Beverly asked as Tyrone and Brenda approached them.

"Tyrone, your timing is perfect. I'm simply curious. Almost a year ago, many of us decided not to support the pastor, so he would quit. But one by one, everyone had a change of heart and became very supportive. The last person to change her position in the pastor's favor was Barbara. I'm just wondering who is blackmailing who? Do you feel like the first lady extorted you?"

Before Tyrone could say anything, Brenda started speaking.

"Wait a minute. I have a story about the first lady to share with you all. It's best to hear it from Willie," Brenda declared as she invited Willie to join the conversation with her, Charlene, Beverly, and Tyrone.

"Yes, what's up?" Willie asked.

"Please tell us the story of the first lady giving you her card then telling your brother to call her."

Willie smiled then began laughing. "You must be joking me."

"Willie, please!"

"Well Brenda talked me into asking my brother, Malcolm, who is a police officer in the Atlanta, Georgia area, to ask someone in Seattle, Washington about the first lady. About a week later, we ran into each other at Home Depot and she asked me if Malcolm Jamal Long was my brother. I said yes, and she replied, 'I heard he's been asking about me, so tell him to call me,' and she handed me a card with her phone number on it. I told my brother and trashed the card."

"The sister is well-connected." Brenda commented.

"Everyone, I'm simply saying someone coerced us into changing our minds. Let's talk about it. Is First Lady Joanne blackmailing everyone?" Charlene asked.

"Do you feel as though she blackmailed you?" Tyrone asked, not wanting to reveal his secrets.

"In some ways," replied Charlene.

Sharon Macy, Church Clerk; Karen Lightfoot, Ministry of Music; and Barbara Power, Vice President of the Trustees noticed Charlene Monk, President of the Health Ministry; Beverly Lot, President of the Culinary Ministry; Tyrone Cummings, President of the Ushers, and Willie Long, Chairman of the Deacons talking, so they went over to join the conversation.

"Can we join you guys?" Karen asked.

"Yes, we're talking about you; the more the better?" Charlene replied.

"What's the topic?" Karen asked.

"I'm curious if anyone feels they've been blackmailed by the first lady?" Charlene asked everyone.

"That's a good question; and yes, I do," Barbara replied.

"What did she say to you?" Tyrone asked as he deflected the attention from himself.

Barbara merely looked at everyone, not wanting to discuss her secrets.

"Must someone say something to be blackmailed?" Karen asked.

James, McDonald, Chairman of the Trustees; George Logan, City Manager; and Jermaine Williams, Chairman of the Board of Directors were having a private conversation when they spotted a larger group of people off to the side, away from the crowd, having a private conversation and decided to join them.

"I think I can guess what this group is talking about?"" James said. "And it's not the pastor's upcoming surprise birthday party," George added.

"How do you know we're all invited?" Travis asked.

"Joanne asked Lori for help; Lori and I work together."

"I must admit, the church has only been blessed since the McCoy's joined us. We're blessed to have them, and I truly love them both," Jermaine proclaimed.

"Well they're here to stay. They're only thirty-five years old. If you're good to them, they will stay for twenty to thirty years," George offered.

"Now here's the question. Does anyone think the first lady blackmailed them? And must a person say something to be blackmailing you?" Charlene asked.

Richard walked up to his wife, Charlene. "Excuse me everyone. Babe, you have a phone call."

Charlene retrieved her cell phone from Richard and he walked away. Charlene took the phone but ignored what her husband said to her as she folded her arms and kept talking.

"Again, I believe she blackmailed many of us or all of us?" Charlene stated emphatically.

"Really, why do you think that?" Willie asked.

"Tyrone, what made you change your position? What about you Sharon, Karen, and you Barbara?" George inquired.

"What made you do an about face?" James asked Willie.

"Joanne McCoy forced me into doing what the pastor wanted from me, as well as each one of you."

"Okay, tell us what she said and what she did?" Willie prompted.

"This is comical, really it is. It's a script taken directly out of the movies…"

Before Jermaine could complete his statement, he was interrupted.

"I hope you're being serious," Beverly interjected.

"Listen to me. In The Godfather II, when Michael Corleone, played by Al Pacino, was in the courtroom sitting next to the brother of the man who was supposed to testify against him in the Corleone's crimes. The man who turned against the Corleone family knew their history – kill or be killed. Now Michael never said he would kill the brother, but because he was sitting beside Michael, the message implied was I own you. You turn on me, I will kill your family," Tyrone stated.

"And how is that connected to us?" James asked.

"We all have skeletons; that's obvious. We're not ready to share them with each other, with anyone. She gave us the impression that she might know things we didn't want revealed. To protect our dark secrets, our own fears and paranoia caused us to do what we thought she wanted us to do. None of us have a clue if she knows anything about any of us, but we're too afraid to risk it. So we all submitted not to her, but to her husband's objectives. In reality, she may not know anything about us. Actually, she may be as dumb as a doorknob concerning our private lives," Charlene admitted.

221

Confession

"The truth of the matter is, if we are truly born again Christians, we wouldn't be concerned with what people think about us. Our purpose and goal in life as a born again Christian is to live and die for Jesus. I think that's the message we all should take from here. The question we all should ask ourselves is – am I a born again Christian. If the answer is yes, we shouldn't be concerned about those that hurt the body, but the ones who can damage both the body and spirit." Barbara Powers proclaimed.

"Do you think you're a born again Christian?" Charlene asked.

"I learned from my weakness that Satan will not take advantage of me again," replied Barbara.

Everyone went on for the next five minutes talking about Joanne McCoy blackmailing them and their faith in Jesus Christ. Nevertheless, no one revealed what they wanted to remain private.

"Charlene, you've been holding that phone for a while. Is someone listening to our conversation?" Tyrone's wife, Brenda, asked.

Charlene brought the phone to her ear and mouth.

"Hello?"

"Charlene, I'm returning your call."

"First Lady!," Charlene shouted

Everyone turned to the side and saw the first lady sitting and eating with her phone to her ear.

"Damn," Charlene uttered as everyone walked away.

The First lady looked up to heaven with a smile on her face and quietly said, "My Lord, My God, you are surely a good and awesome GOD."

#####

38219124R00131

Made in the USA
Lexington, KY
28 December 2014